The Color Picture Guide to Extraterrestrials

Author: Neil Fontaine
Illustrator: Neil Fontaine
Editor: Jennifer Ratliff

Published by Neil Fontaine

ISBN 978-0-615-18910-9

Contents

Preface

The night glowed brilliantly; stars scattered amongst every clear space of sky, while the brisk wind seemed to blow the inspiration into my already-enlightened thoughts. On the sketch pad in front of me, in subdued form, the drawn figure of the Reptilian said, "Are you certain that you have caught a true glimpse of my people?"

I stood quickly, suddenly afraid. Though I had imagined this moment in many dreams, this seemed hardly the setting for an extraterrestrial visit.

"What images do I have to draw on?" I said.

"True," the Reptilian admitted. "Certainly some research would lead you to a more valid representation."

At that point, I shot into action. With the urge to know how other artists had painted Reptilians in the past, I scoured the local library, the half-price bookstore down the street, and the New Age shop across town, finding nothing but crude drawings. Sure, there were decent paintings of extraterrestrials in the science-fiction comics, but I knew these were not based on eyewitness accounts or personal experience.

I prepared to return home, wondering if the drawing I drew could be a Reptilian's true form, or if I too had drawn from a creative subconscious. At the used book store down the road from my home, I finally ran across a book that offered promise of some kind of realism. *Barlowe's Guide to Extraterrestrials: Great Aliens from Science Fiction Literature*, by Wayne Douglas Barlowe, purely admitted its origins—yet, the images shown were full color paintings, not simply sketches.

I returned home inspired both by what I had found and what I hadn't. I had found a good collection of alien paintings, but I had not found a painting based on actual human accounts of visitations or eyewitness accounts. Hence this book.

For years I had studied ancient texts that spoke of aliens visiting ancient man. Using books such as the Hebrew Bible, *Epic of Gilgamesh*, *The Mahabharata*, *Srimad Bhagavatam*, *Ramayana*, *Vedas* and other Hindu texts, Mayan myths, Sumerian myths, Greek myths, African myths, and even Native American myths, I could now piece some of that puzzle together. With modern abduction and contactee stories to supplement the information I already had, I began to see a pattern of truth emerge. I returned home to the sketch of the Reptilian sitting on my student's desk and waited for the drawing to speak to me as it had before. The Reptilian remained silent, but looking into the eyes that I had drawn, I saw a gleam reminiscent of a wink. "You're on the right track," it told me, and that was all I needed.

The information that I have built my life around, particularly that in evolution, astronomy, physics and other hard sciences, allows me to hypothesize how life on other planets may have evolved, and how alien species from these worlds have also evolved. In the following pages I will provide the reader with information regarding species' technological achievements, as well as details on their physical attributes, diet, reproduction, habitat, and social structure

This book is meant as an introduction to the many different life-forms that inhabit the universe. For Ufologists, it is data that can be used to corroborate contact stories. For scientists, it is knowledge of advanced civilizations. For the artist, a template that can be used to properly represent alien beings. Finally, for the avid student of life, it is knowledge that can motivate and inspire one to do something to further humankind's advancement into the universal scope of intelligence.

Chapter 1: Alternative Theory of Evolution

I pinned the reptilian drawing above my desk to remind me of the fallacy of human thought, the belief that only one bipedal creature with an intelligent brain could exist in the universe. It's hard to think beyond Earth when the practical act of surviving takes precedence over discovery and enlightenment. Nevertheless, so it is. For now, I had to focus on putting the pieces of knowledge together that years of study have led to. Evolution was my first target.

We are all familiar with Darwin's Theory of Natural Selection: organisms with traits that help them survive and produce more offspring thrive, while those organisms that cannot adapt or are too weak to mate effectively die off. For a good refresher on the subject, the University of California's Museum of Paleontology maintains a wonderful site on evolution, http://evolution.berkeley.edu.

My Theory

When I started this book just a week before, I made it a point to ignore the brief speaking episode between me and the drawing. I continued to live life as one might expect. I ran errands, spent time with my child and wife, and watched movies after a long day at work. But tonight, behind the humdrum of house activity, I found myself explaining the tenants of my alternative theory of evolution to this imaginary alien.

"I subscribe to an alternate theory of evolution, one that answers difficult questions and explains how species come to exist in the first place. It also attempts to surmise the existence and evolution of alien species such as the Grays, the alien species that most humans depict in film."

"How do you propose to prove that your belief is any different than what is already out there?"

Although most people would have been surprised if their artwork suddenly spoke, it wasn't as unnerving as it could have been.

"First, it is not a belief, it is a scientific theory," I said defensively. "A belief is purely philosophical. Second, my version of evolution is different."

In my mind, the reptilian scoffed.

"I await an explanation," he said. "What is the difference between a scientific theory and a philosophical theory?"

I thought about defining a theory to him as "a set of statements or principles devised to explain a group of facts or phenomena, especially one that has been repeatedly tested or is widely accepted and can be used to make predictions about natural phenomena."[1] But I chose a simpler way to explain it. Sometimes I forgot that I was dealing with intelligence at least as powerful as my own.

"Let's take a philosopher, for example. He says, 'I have a theory about why the devil is so evil.' But his use of the word theory can't hold a candle to a scientific theory that researchers can challenge qualitatively."

"Yes," the alien responded thoughtfully. "After all, does not a philosopher deal in thoughts, which are not quantitative?"

"Right," I agreed. "Another example of philosophical theory is a person who states that life was created six thousand years ago. The physical evidence clearly refutes that claim, which leads me to ask: What scientific basis could such a 'theory' have, if science itself denies it?"

"Yes," said the alien again, this time with a little glimmer in his eye.

"What, do you have evidence to the contrary?"

"It is against the common rules of the universe to reveal its secrets. Therefore, I plead the fifth, as you would say."

"Okay," I said, bewildered by this being that didn't really exist but was nonetheless leading the conversation. I quickly continued the speech.

"A scientific theory, on the other hand, uses clearly identifiable and quantitative data to explain a process or event. The data is placed with known laws and incorporated into already-existing theories. Because the evidence is observable, scientific theory relies on fact, rather than beliefs, about what happens in the universe.

Based on observable phenomena, my theory is easy to categorize and incorporate into already-established theories. Therefore, it is a valid scientific theory."

"I believe it is time that you reveal your theory, unless you fear that I will debate its validity."

"No, not at all," I scoffed. "My theory is that convergent evolution on our planet is evidence that everything evolves the same everywhere, according to the same rules. In other words, evolution is universally equal. Therefore, we shouldn't expect alien life, uh—you—to be very different from humans. If another planet has similar pressure and temperature, intelligent life there should look very similar to intelligent life here."

"Very interesting, quite so," the reptilian said. I glanced at the drawing, half-expecting to see him nod his head in agreement. Instead, the light from the lit hallway crept through the door, making his form look ruddy, more indistinct. I stood up and stretched in the darkness. I had spent hours in here conversing with an alien voice in my head. I quickly turned the computer on and turned into words what I had been thinking the past hours. Then I stopped. In order for readers to understand my theory, I realized that I would need to provide at least basic information on DNA and evolution. My fingers already tired, I started to type again.

DNA and Evolution

In many ways, evolution is misunderstood. In particular, the concept of randomness versus physical laws presents readers with a confusing conundrum. The evolution website of The University of California says this:

> "Variation is random, selection usually is not. Selection of favorable traits within a population occurs when living things meet all the challenges presented to them. Physical laws and not a random process govern the pressures, although it might appear to be so. Barring the occasional tree randomly falling on an organism, or a volcano wiping out a population, selection is not random and evolution does not happen by chance."

The key to evolution is that minute changes in genetic material results in the formation of entirely new variations of life; hence, DNA, which is the genetic instructor of life, plays the largest role in evolution. DNA, also known as deoxyribonucleic acid, is "a nucleic acid that carries the genetic information in the cell and is capable of self-replication and synthesis of RNA." [2] DNA is not a single molecule, but a pair of molecules joined by hydrogen bonds. Each strand of DNA is actually a chain of nucleotides, which are the chemical building blocks of the universe. There are four types of nucleotides, called adenine (A), cystosine (C), guanine (G), and thymine (T). In some organisms, Uracil (U) will replace thymine, and these "combine" with each other in specific ways. Adenine always combines with thymine, and cystosine only mates with guanine. Therefore, all life as we know it is a combination of these base pairs, with occasional substitutions of Uracil for thymine.

It may be hard to believe that every human being on Earth is composed of variations of these simple molecules. But consider: everything that you see on your computer, whether it is e-mail, graphics, pictures or video, is a combination of only two numbers, 1 and 0. In addition, the entire universe together is composed of only 92 different kinds of elements (plus 20 elements that are man-made). Therefore, all that you see around you, both on Earth and in space, is a result of the combination of those basic elements.

To illustrate the variance allowed by DNA structure, consider that the difference in the sequence order between our DNA and a banana is 50%. A simple change of guanine to cystosine can result in an entirely new species of animal. Therefore, it is not as far-fetched as some might believe to think that these different orientations are universal, and could result in an entirely new species of humanoid.

Survival of the Fittest

One of the tenets of evolution is the idea of "survival of the fittest," otherwise known as natural selection. Natural selection helps species adapt to their environments. Other important aspects of evolution are anomalies and homologies. Homology is how two species share a trait that they inherited from a common ancestor. Anomalies occur when two or more species share a trait that they developed independently. In the following examples, I will focus on the concept of the anomaly. To read about one of the examples provided, follow the links provided at the end of the chapter.

1. Barnacles and limpets are sea creatures that have hard shells for protection. However, the barnacle has a shrimp-like body while limpets have a snail-like body. They both evolved shells independently, which means that they didn't receive the trait from a common ancestor. The laws of natural selection resulted in two species that are unrelated, yet share the same trait.[3]

2. Squirrels and sugar gliders have both separately evolved a flap of skin between the legs and arms for gliding from tree to tree.[4]

3. The similarities between the plants Hoodia and Cholla clearly developed individually. While they both have thick, water-filled branches and sharp spines, Hoodia is native to South Africa, while Cholla is native to North American deserts.[5]

4. The shark and the dolphin each have a dorsal fin, flippers and a torpedo-shaped body. However, the dolphin and shark are obviously not related. Sharks are cold-blooded, while dolphins are warm-blooded. In addition, the shark existed 450 million years ago, while scientists have traced the dolphin's beginning as a species to only 50 million years ago.[6]

Convergent Evolution and Alternative Views

The concept of convergent evolution is based on anomaly; species that are evolutionarily unrelated manage to develop the same traits due to similar lifestyles and selection pressures. This is the reason that both bats and birds, which are unrelated, have wings. It is not such a stretch to consider that two humanoid species separated by light years might share a similar appearance. Planets all form according to the same physical laws. This means that somewhere there are planets that are similar to planet Earth. If these planets followed a similar physical change over time, it is only natural to imagine that life would have evolved in a similar fashion. The theory of convergent evolution hypothesizes the existence of humanoid creatures on other Earth-like planets, simply because life on Earth-like planets would likely have similar lifestyles.

From what we know about evolution, this kind of similarity is the norm, rather than coincidence. In fact, when considering the art of camouflage and species "copying" other species to avoid predation, it almost seems as if natural selection is its own intelligence. If traits develop by sheer intuition, how much of a stretch is it to think that humanoid species, under the same environmental stresses as are on Earth, could develop on planets that are much further away?

Notes

1. According to Wikipedia.com, **theory** definition
2. *The American Heritage® Dictionary of the English Language*, Fourth Edition. Copyright © 2000 by Houghton Mifflin Company.

3. http://evolution.berkeley.edu/evolibrary/article/side_0_0/analogy_01
4. http://evolution.berkeley.edu/evolibrary/article/side_0_0/analogy_02
5. http://evolution.berkeley.edu/evolibrary/article/side_0_0/analogy_03
6. http://evolution.berkeley.edu/evolibrary/article/side_0_0/analogy_04

Chapter 2: Classification System

The edges of my drawing started to curl up, revealing the constant passage of time. It had been only a few weeks since the reptilian drawing began speaking to me, and yet I remained remarkably sane. We'd had a few conversations, the figment of my imagination and I, but today the being threw me yet another curveball.

"You do realize that I am real, don't you?"

"Sure," I said, thinking quite the opposite.

"My name is Azazel. I represent the life that doesn't originate on Earth."

I stood with my mouth open and eyebrows pinched for a moment, wondering if I had finally snapped, or if something incomprehensible was happening.

"And how many of you are there?" I asked in a tone that is more sarcastic than I wanted.

"There are more intelligent bipedal species in the universe than there are Earthlings such as you."

I gave a nervous chuckle. His comment was a jab at the human race and our ego from thousands of years of supremacy. I changed the subject quickly.

"So, these species—are they related? Do they all come from one ancient ancestor, like we believe about our species?"

This time Azazel chuckled. "Perhaps if you shared with me this 'ancient ancestor' theory, because I am not what you would call a scientist."

"Yes, sorry, I assumed—"

"That I could read your mind? Not all of us do, just as only a few here on Earth can read minds."

I blushed, embarrassed at my naïve thoughts, but curious.

"How is it then that I am speaking with you now, if you are not in my mind?"

Azazel offered a sly smile. "Let us not get ahead of ourselves. I shall explain all that in good time. Please, back to our discussion?"

"Yes," I murmured, and flipped the switch on my laptop. I opened Word and began typing.

Classification Explained

In the eighteenth century, Carolus Linnaeus grouped Earth species together according to shared physical characteristics. However, modern taxonomy relies on common descent. The names given to species are often in Latin or Greek, which make them sound scientific, until you find out what the words mean. One example is the phrase *Homo sapiens,* which is Latin for "wise man." Other examples of the simplicity of our "scientific" naming system are these:

Synapsids: "fused arch," *aka* Theropsids, "beast arch," the mammal-like reptiles.

Sauropsid: "lizard face," the class of mostly egg-laying vertebrate animals, including all of the modern and ancient reptiles, excluding Synapsids.

Tetrapods: Greek for "four-legged."

Selachimorpha: Latin for "form of cartilaginous fish." This super order includes sharks.

As you can see, naming species is not rocket science. Actually, it is quite silly to imagine what scientific lectures would sound like if professors had to use the English equivalents of the species they studied.

You may be wondering what I was talking about when I called Sauropsid a class, and Selachimorpha a super order. Many of us might not remember much of what we learned in biology classes, so let's look at how scientists divide animals into species. We will use humans and chimpanzees as our reference subjects.

Classifications	Humans	Chimpanzees
Kingdom	Animalia (L) "animal"	Animalia
Phylum	Cordata (L) "cord, string"	Cordata
Class	Mammalia (L) "breast"	Mammalia
Order	Primates (L) "of the first"	Primates
Family	Hominidae (L) "Men"	Hominidae
Subfamily	Homininae (L) "men"	Homininae
Tribe	Hominini (L) "men"	Hominini
Subtribe	Hominina (L) "men"	Paninina (L) "hanging flaps ofofof skin"
Genus	Homo (L) "man"	Pan
Species	Homo sapiens "wise man"	Pan troglodytes (L) "cave dwellers"

This taxonomy chart allows you to follow the evolution of both species up to the point that they split off from a common ancestor in the sub-tribe category.

It is interesting to note that the word "Hominidae," which means "men" in Latin, includes not only humans but chimpanzees, gorillas, and orangutans. Similarly, Homininae, man's sub-family, includes some of man's extinct ancestors, such as Australopithecus. The tribe has the same word origin and includes the same animals (including humans).

Homo sapiens are the only existing species in the Hominina sub-tribe. They are characterized by a progression of increasingly erect bipedal locomotion. Fossil records indicate that Homo sapiens split from our common ancestor with the Chimpanzees about three to five million years ago.

My task done, I looked to Azazel for a sign that he was listening. He stared ahead, just as I drew him, and again I wondered if this is all in my mind.

"Do you want to hear how I have categorized extraterrestrial life?"

He didn't answer, so I took the liberty of elaborating in case he was listening.

"As my theory surmises that life should have evolved similarly throughout the universe, I should be able to classify all extraterrestrial life just as scientists on Earth classify all animals. Therefore, I have combined the information from the ancient texts with modern cases about extraterrestrials. Because of our scientific knowledge of evolution, I have been able to hypothesize the origin of extraterrestrial species."[1]

He grinned but did not respond, so I continued.

"My taxonomy is based on how the species evolved. I stay as true to traditional scientific classification as possible, using Latin for the divisions. I have outlined in my chapter on evolution how life throughout the universe evolves according to the same laws. This is why I use many of the same Phylums, Classes, and Orders, even though many of the species evolved on other planets."

Azazel yawned, and stalked toward the door.

"This is all very interesting," he said, "but I must be going."

Chapter 3: Theories About Hybrids

Since beginning my project, I had received more than a little flak from the family about my marathon "writing" sessions, although they didn't know about Azazel. I framed the drawing last week to keep time from doing any more of its damage, and tonight I stared blandly at the drawing, wanting to go to bed. Azazel, who had been expecting me to arrive for our discussions every night, asked quickly where I had been. Usually slow to argue, tonight I was short-tempered.

"I have responsibilities here that you will never understand," I blurted. Azazel's eyes darkened, and for the first time I saw a hint of the supremacy he must feel. Without waiting for him to mention such a fact, I shrugged.

"Why did you come to me, then?"

Azazel gave a smile that hinted at something more, but I wasn't in the mood to pursue it, and he soon shrugged it off as well.

"We are not that much different, underneath it all," he said.

"How do you figure that?" I said, anticipating the answer.

"Your blood courses through my veins," he said, apparently reveling in the shock-value of his comment. "I am not pure-bred."

For ages, the debate has been raging about the "hybrid" question. Do aliens actually impregnate women, then come back and steal their babies at birth?

"You can't tell me that all those crazy stories are true?" I asked, trying not to sound incredulous.

"And why would they not be true? Do you not "interbreed" similar species here to increase genetic strength or desirability?"

"With pets," I admitted. "But not a dominant species—"

"Who says you are dominant?" Azazel snapped, and I stood dumbfounded for a moment, whisked to confusion by his sudden tirade.

"We ARE the dominant species," I said.

"Here," he added.

"Yes, we are the dominant species on Earth."

"Is that what you believe?" Azazel asked.

I could see that he was simply trying to challenge me today, and at first, I let the comment go. However, I soon returned to it out of curiosity.

"If humans are not the dominant species on Earth, than what are, dolphins?" It was a joke from a popular science fiction story, but he didn't look amused.

"Do you know how long intelligent life has been visiting your planet? Do you even realize? We were here when the species you call dinosaurs roamed the planet. We lost many of our kind when Object 3L664B5 hit your—our planet."

"Are you talking about the asteroid that scientists believe caused the extinction of the dinosaurs 65 million years ago?"

Azazel stopped. After a minute of silence, his features rippled. "I must go," he said suddenly. I could feel him leaving; a glance at the drawing showed a glimmer and then solid ink and shades, once again two-dimensional.

"Wait!" I yelled, wondering what could have caused such a quick retreat.

I didn't have much time to wonder. The night was going fast, and I still had a lot to cover. He brought up a subject that I had thought about quite a bit since I began studying the interactions between humans and extraterrestrials.

Life as a hybrid

The idea of the human-alien hybrid is nothing new, but the reasoning behind the intermingling of our species is as varied as the ethnicities on Earth. Below is a summary of many of the common beliefs that researchers hold regarding the reason for creating an alien-human hybrid:

Possible reason #1: Lack of lower job placement

To replace artificial intelligence as assembly workers. In an advanced civilization, menial labor is considered sub-standard. By building a society of hybrids, it creates another race of "intelligent" beings both capable of such menial positions and oblivious to their societal position. Humans by themselves would be too hard to train to complete such tasks; however, hybrids have the mental capacity of the more supreme beings while maintaining no such disgrace of small tasks.

While this seems ridiculous, it already happens on Earth. Middle-class society often completes tasks that are "below" the consideration of those with a higher income, but are also too complex or require too much education for members of the lower class to complete.

Possible Reason #2: To prolong life

In order to prolong life, aliens found a way to download their memories into a computer, which they then downloaded on a nightly basis. As the body's natural reaction to time is to decay, they also cloned their bodies so that when the body died, someone could re-download its memories into the clone. Unfortunately, after so many times of transferring their memories into clones, the mind became fragile and broke down from an overload of memories. Insanity often resulted from this overload. Hybrids, whose brains cannot fully integrate each memory, remain sane, and this has helped alien intelligence to continue its existence.

Possible Reason #3: To create new experiences

Aliens have become so self-aware that they can only experience spiritual growth through integrating with minds not of their own species. However, their memories are not compatible with the human body. Therefore, they created a hybrid, a cross between alien and human, where they could download their memories and experience human existence more freely.

Possible reason #4: To experience the role of nurturing parent or caregiver

Having cloned themselves so much, aliens have become so genetically similar that they can no longer create "normal" children. In order to further their race, and experience what it is like to be a caregiver, they created hybrids, creating a mixture of DNA from their race and human beings. This is closely linked to another reason that creating a hybrid might be beneficial, and this is strictly to keep their species from going extinct because of disease. It is genetic diversity that makes the body strong against disease and genetic problems. Unfortunately, it will be this genetic diversity that causes the intelligent species to evolve backwards, as hybrids do not have the same mental capacity as their full-blooded cousins.

An X-file analogy

Some X-file addicts may say that aliens are making hybrids in order to take over the world. The problem with this idea is one of logic. Why wouldn't the species have simply taken over the world already? They have both the intelligence and technology to do as they wish among barbarians such as humans. Why breed with less supreme beings?

Intelligent life has been visiting humans since ancient times. Well-documented proof shows that their visitations resulted in a sudden change in religion; if they had wanted the human race destroyed, they would have done so then, either through sickness or through other means.

It is conceivable that hybrids live among us, as congressional representatives, presidents, and country leaders. According to the ancient texts, hybrids can make themselves look human, particularly the Naga, or snake-men.

A New Twist

Azazel returned to me, this time not in the drawing, but in my dreams. He did not speak of the reason behind his quick departure, but hinted that there might have been something more than a mere asteroid responsible for the extinction of the dinosaurs.

It was then that it occurred to me that the painting I had been working on was accurate. He looked mostly human, but with a green-brown tint to his skin. His cheek bones were high, almost running into his lower eyes.

"I was created in a laboratory, not unlike your 'test-tube' children," he said. "My female bore me here on Earth . . . in a place with golden fields. I was taken soon after."

For the first time since meeting him, I could feel the emotion in his voice.

"So, your mother was human?"

"I am not proud of my station. However, it is for the best."

"What exactly is your "station? What would you rather be doing?" I asked.

"Since the 1940's I have been around your planet talking to people just like you, people who are not in the highest station, nor the lowest. I was commissioned to speak to people like you about the future. About our arrival."

"You mean there are actually aliens coming to Earth?"

Azazel offered a sly smirk. "We are already here, my friend. Purebreds, hybrids, genetic mixtures of all varieties. Only those who can pass as human walk among you, but . . . the others are here."

"Really," I said with a smirk of my own. I couldn't get the image of the famed Men In Black out of my mind. "No warships? No heat rays? How do you expect to take over the Earth?"

Azazel didn't smile. "We don't wish to "take over" the Earth. Our goal is simply to bring you to a more advanced plane of social awareness."

I was tiring of this dream and this debate.

"Well, you're not doing a very good job. You've had, what, thousands of years here on Earth and we haven't changed."

Azazel's body shimmered—darkened and returned to muted green-brown in a matter of seconds.

"Ignorant human," he said. "We have not even arrived yet."

"You just said that—" I began.

"I said that our kind has been here for many years. Visitors, stranded. It is not our position to change the way you think. That is the task of a far greater intelligence than mine. It is my station to introduce humans to the idea of an alien presence, to prepare you for the dignitaries. Thanks to us, you speak freely of life on other planets. Generations before you had no such luxuries. When the first fleet arrives in the next century, you will be ready."

"They will not receive a warm welcome," I spouted. "We will fight for what is ours."

I had been wishing for alien contact for many years, but I had always hoped there would be a sense of brotherhood between us, not pity.

Azazel grew quiet. "This is precisely why you need us. Your mind cannot grasp a world that is not in your possession. You would rather destroy it than share it. Such children, you humans are."

"I would like to talk to one of these "dignitaries," I said, my insides boiling. "Humans won't stand for being insulted. We are not children to be coddled and told how to act. We have earned our place in the Universe."

Azazel turned his back to me. "Perhaps I should not be the one talking to you of such things. My own humanity craves argument. I shall leave now."

There was no time to ask him back. He disappeared as quickly as a bubble that touches a child's finger. I snapped awake, aware that I had lost something important in my life.

Chapter 4: Weapons

I went to bed angry. After everything I had given up to meet Azazel, all the arguments I had started with my loved ones over spending so much time at the computer, it had ended with nothing.

As I drifted off, I had strange thoughts, images of alien invasions with ray guns and men in spacesuits firing back. If I'd been any more awake, the images would have been funny. As it was, I felt the tossing and turning of a bad night sleep beginning, and fell asleep thinking of alien weapons.

When I woke up it was as clear to me as if someone had downloaded the information into my brain while I was sleeping. I glanced at Azazel; he was not there of course, only the penned drawing I had created months ago. Was it my imagination, or did I see a soft grin? *Write it down*, it seemed to say. *I gave you what you need.*

Some Hindu texts mentioned weapons used by extraterrestrials, but I could not be sure which of those were made up by Hindus and which were original. So I discarded those and moved on to trying to explain the range of intelligent weapons.

There are two classes and three sub-classes of weapons. The first class is mind weapons, the second is physical weapons, and these physical weapons come in two varieties: those controlled by physical touch and those controlled by the mind.

To manipulate matter with your thoughts is mind power. It sounds like something possible only in the realm of unicorns and elves, but mind power is not supernatural; it is as natural as the ability to think. Keep in mind, however, that mind powers are not magic. Magic is a thing of movies and backstreet stages. Mind powers are real and visible on a daily basis. Monks have demonstrated in experiments the ability to raise their temperature, raise or lower their heart rate, and raise or lower their blood pressure. The fact is that we do not understand what thought is and is not capable of. For instance, dolphins can send sound waves with their thoughts that stun larger fish.

A new study has shown that humans can sense the emotions of other humans on one level or another. People who are autistic, however, do not feel emotions as others do, whether happiness, fear or grief. This may be why people often judge them to be unfeeling. Sociopaths may also have this problem.

The Gist of Psychic Development

Everything is composed of energy. Because of this, there is no reason to believe that our thoughts, which are the result of combined energy, cannot manipulate energy. That means that the things you hear about in the movies mind reading, mind control, telepathy, telekinesis, and yes, even the mental power of seduction are all possible. So what are all of these "gifts?"

- Mind reading: The ability to search the thoughts and memories of others.
- Mind control: The ability to control another life form, which is to get to them to do things they are not fully aware of, or otherwise would not do. This is not easy to do, especially if you run into a person who has the same ability, as they can simply block your attempts.
- Telepathy: The ability to talk to others using thoughts instead of words. This is a two-way highway. If only one person has telepathy then he can send his thoughts to another, but that person cannot answer back mentally.
- Telekinesis: The ability to move objects with just thoughts.
- Seduction: The ability to seduce someone to do something he or she normally would not do. This includes attracting a partner who might not physically desire you.
- Power to will: the ability to do things that you normally would not think possible. Examples would be super strength, super speed, super agility, and so forth. Someone might even be able to prevent themselves from burning while walking through fire.

Each of these powers uses the brain in its raw form, without conscious manipulation. The brain interprets what the eyes see. It processes information that is presented through sight. Hence the saying "seeing is believing." It takes a little less than a second for the information our eyes see to travel to the part of our brain that interprets that information. Therefore, it is not much of a stretch to think that if we could modify the time it took for the brain to interpret information, or if we could modify what our eyes perceive, we could manipulate the brain. Often what we interpret seeing is not what our eyes perceived anyway. An example would be playing a video clip of two men arguing to a college class and then asking them to figure out what the two men were arguing over and why. In the middle of the argument, a man dressed up like a bear does a little dance in the background, then leaves. Most of the students would never notice the bear. Their eyes perceived the bear but their brains deleted it because it was not important to the task that of finding out what the men were arguing about.

The implications of this technology are grand. Subliminal messaging aside, you could train the brain not to process certain information. For those with the technology, it wouldn't be that hard to interfere with how the brain interprets what a person's eyes perceive; hypothetically, you could be a reptilian yet fool the brain into processing your image as very human.

Psychic powers also have a lot to do with how weapons will develop in the future. In many advanced civilizations, the human brain will connect with Nano-bot technology to create weapons more deadly than a thousand neutron bombs, and yet so precise that those who aren't targeted won't even know anything happened.

Nano-bots are an important tool to an advanced civilization. These microscopic robots can assemble and disassemble virtually any object atom by atom. Nano-bots can remove pollution from air, water, dirt, or anything else, making it pure. If you broke a bone, Nano-bots could put it back together in seconds. Nano-bots can build food, houses, cars, etc. They can remove cancer, viruses, bacteria and so forth. They can also kill.

The Brahma weapon is an example of one that utilizes Nano-bot technology, and it is described in ancient Hindu texts. This staff weapon appears only when you chant a mantra. The mantra is the password that causes the Nano-bots to build the weapon out of available atoms. The Brahma weapon shoots a powerful blast of energy that can destroy a whole city according to the Hindu texts, but it is only as powerful as the person wielding it. Fortunately, the average person could not operate the weapon, since it requires the mantra and the right level of mind control.

Other weapons that intelligent life may use are swords that remind one of the light sabers in Star Wars, except this high-energy sword only works with thought power.

Chapter 5: Creation Story

I awoke in a bright room, lying on a bed that reminded me of my stay in the hospital. I was afraid to open my eyes, because I didn't want to know if I was dead. There was such an intense light, yet the air chilled me to the bones.

I formed a temporary visor with my hands and looked at the floor. It appeared to absorb the light. I reached my fingers to the floor, and though they didn't touch, I sensed the soft yet stiff texture of its surface. I traced the floor with my fingers. As my arm straightened, my fingers limply pointed to a door. A figure resembling a man approached me.

"Who are you," I said, my eyes squinted. "Where am I?"

"You asked to see the dignitaries," he said without words.

"Where am I?" The air seemed to swallow my words.

His hand, which was as smooth as a baby's, grabbed my wrist gently. He coaxed me to follow him. I slid off the bed and followed without a thought. I didn't feel fear, but a sense of curiosity and wonder.

When we reached the door, it dissipated as if the being had commanded it to do so. As we walked down the hallway, it occurred to me that I could not smell anything. It wasn't like getting used to an odor. There was just no smell at all.

We traveled the darkened hallway. It wasn't a pitch black; the walls glowed an eerie orange. It reminded me of being inside a ribbed vacuum cleaner hose, made with transparent rubber. I could see through to a series of blue-segmented rings, each a few feet from the other. I focused past the tubing.

"My God," I said, too quickly to stop myself. We were in space!

I composed myself enough to take in my surroundings. Now that my eyes had adjusted to the darkness, I could see the man guiding me. I felt uneasy with the dim light gleaming off his large bald head. At first, I thought he was naked, but then realized his clothing, which was almost fused to his body, was the same color as his pale skin. His long, thin fingers were still loosely gripping my wrist. We reached the end of the hallway, and another door. Again, we floated through unimpeded. This room was bright, but not blindingly so. The ceiling and floor curved around me, and I almost felt like I had walked into a large pearly-colored almond.

Another figure with the same appearance was in the room. I couldn't tell if he was staring at me or through me. I was almost lost in the parallel voids of his large eyes.

I had many questions. Thoughts roiled through my head like an angry wave, but once again, the only words I could muster were like those of a child.

"Who are you; where am I?"

"You have requested to communicate with us."

"That doesn't answer my question!"

"You have ascertained that you have entered space; however, the precise coordinates are of no importance."

They seemed distant, yet somehow comforting and graceful.

"We have not much time. Therefore, we now impart to you knowledge concerning the origin of things."

They had a peaceful presence that made me comfortable enough to ask, "Alright, but could you talk more normal?"

They stared into each others' black voids as if puzzled, and then the one standing beside me spoke.

"Yes, we can manage."

The being in front of me, who seemed to be standing a bit taller than my "escort," continued,

"What you presently call the universe is but one of many ultra-galaxies. Each ultra-galaxy goes through a stage of expansion and then collapse. I believe your scientists refer to this as the "big-bang" and "big-crunch."

He beckoned me to sit.

"The actual universe is comprised of many ultra-galaxies, some in the state of expansion and others in the state of collapse. Our ultra-galaxy that you call the universe is in the state of expansion."

"So what we call the universe is *not* the universe?"

"Correct. After one ultra-galaxy's collapse, our ultra-galaxy started to expand. On a planet that we can refer to as Alternoanima, the first life forms evolved. Nine billion years ago, the first hominoid developed a philosophy. One of his descendents concluded that there must be an eternal intelligence ultimately claiming responsibility for all life."

I began to open my mouth to question the philosophy comment, but the air absorbed my words as before.

"In time," the head intelligence continued, "His descendents developed advanced technology, squandering the resources they had; similar to what your species is doing on Earth. The people living on Alternoanima, however, dedicated their full attention to the matter instead of allowing one voice to control the fate of the planet."

Again I opened my mouth to argue, but could not speak. I did, however, witness an exchange of gestures from one being to the other that looked a little bit like a friend telling another friend to shut up.

"Several scientists began to work on finding a solution to the global problem, and invented the nano-bot, which you should be familiar with from a popular science fiction television show."

My escort gestured to the wall in front of him. It morphed into a screen. Before I could properly react, an old episode of Star Trek popped up on the screen.

"In this entertainment piece, crew members would often request an item from a utility box. Only moments later their favorite food appeared. This is an example of nano-bots in action. These miniscule robots cleaned the pollution in Alternoanima's air, provided food, and rebuilt the planet. "

The alien made finger gestures and the screen faded back into a wall. "nano-bots were placed in the water, because this provided them with a means to enter the body. Once inside, the nano-bots took on the role of an extra immune system. If one got sick, a nano-bot would disassemble the disease atom by atom. If one broke a bone, the nano-bots stitched it back together. If one got cut—it could continue this way indefinitely."

"So, the nano-bots took away disease, disabilities, injuries . . ."

I was surprised to hear my voice. They must have decided that I could now ask questions.

"Without such worries, the Alternoanimans could focus on learning more advanced technology. They harnessed the power of the sun and began to explore the galaxy; eventually they transformed other planets so that they could live on them.

"Most non-Earth intelligences follow a caste system. They contain warriors, scientists, inventors, artists, and the Un-named. In the case of Alternoanima, the warrior caste altered their DNA to become stronger and bigger. Humans have called these beings by many names, including Anunnaki, Nephilim, Danavas, and Titans."

"Is this supposed to be history, or are you just throwing hypotheticals out there?"

My escort seemed to smile. "It is what you believe it is, until you can see for yourself."

"Some of the scientists," the other being continued without missing a beat, "settled on a planet with gravity four to five times greater than that on your planet. They attached intelligent chips to their brains which changed the way they evolved."

"Why would they do that? How?" I asked.

"They built the chips using neurons and nano-tubes that allowed the higher-frequency computer chips to interface with the lower-frequency brain waves. The chips made it possible to download lots of information and access it as naturally as you might access information stored in your brain, such as a new language, mathematics, or physics."

"I want a brain chip," I blurted.

"As you wish," the leader responded quickly. He walked over to the far wall, wiggled his fingers, and part of the wall opened. He pulled out a sharp instrument and glanced at me.

"It will only hurt a little."

I felt myself grow faint. I must have appeared as scared as I felt, for the two aliens gazed at each other; their stomach muscles fluttered. *Are they laughing?* I thought. The alien at the wall put the tool back and moved to the exact spot he had been in before.

"At first the scientists found it difficult to move on the planet without the aid of anti-gravity technology, because their muscles were used to a weaker gravity field. In time, of course, they adapted. They evolved into what your people call "the Grays." Their fingers thinned to adapt to their work with delicate technology. Their brains became larger and developed two more parts. Their skulls increased in size to harness the larger brain. Their body structure changed, the spine moving more towards the center of the skull to balance the weight of their larger head."

"How does such a skinny neck support such a large head?" I asked, sure that at any point my questions would become offensive.

The aliens appeared to "laugh" again, although I saw no movement of the facial muscles and heard no sound. I only saw their abdomens flutter.

"The muscles in their necks are much denser than yours."

"These Grays, do they believe in God?"

"They have no belief in God; they turned to technology long ago to expand their lives as long as possible. Even against scrutiny, the scientists continued their experiments. They invented technology that could store memories. Each night they downloaded their memories into a device. When death approached, the scientists cloned themselves so that when they did die, their memories would transfer to their new bodies. They thought that they would live forever, but their plan was flawed. They didn't know, they could not have known that the brain is not capable of storing so many lives, so many memories, and emotions. Within a thousand years madness sets in."

"Then what happened to Uncle George?" I quipped.

The two aliens went silent. My escort turned his head toward mine, and I felt him drawing me into his black eyes.

I dropped my eyes to the floor. "Never—never mind," I stuttered. Obviously, they didn't understand sarcasm. "Continue, please."

"The scientists went to work on the problem. The solution was to build a virtual reality device, making it possible to for the beings to live an alternative life. This gave the brain a rest from normal existence. After living about 80 years in the virtual reality device, they were refreshed. However, they found that it wasn't long before madness began to set in again. This would require another sojourn in virtual reality, and soon the time between real and virtual became so small that it was no longer an effective solution. Killing them was the only alternative."

"They were murdered?!"

"It was painless, I guarantee you. And they were aware of the necessity. They were simply put to sleep."

"Have you figured a way to fix things?"

"No, we have not solved this problem."

The leader seemed annoyed at my escort's admittance.

"Six billion years ago," the leader said, his voice louder. "A homo-reptilian species evolved on a distant planet. The African Zulu Shamans called it Imbulu or Chitauli. These beings had scaly skin and some of them had a third eye, tinted red; others had a crown of horns around their heads. These beings were jealous of the intelligence and technology the Grays had, so they mixed the Grays' DNA with their own in the hopes that they would become as smart as the more intelligent Grays. They did not have much success. Instead, they built a new being atom by atom. You can call it Syn, short for Synthetic. It is not an anomaly that your Christian term "sin" and the "syn" being share the same name."

I watched the alien's abdominal muscles ripple, and I wondered if this was his attempt at humor.

"Syn is a grotesque, larger-headed species that resembles us in appearance. Your eyewitnesses often see them with three long fingers, and they float rather than walk above the ground. They use antigravity devices to do this. Although they are built to resemble a biological being, they are more similar to artificial intelligence. They show little to no emotion.

"The Syn are all about efficiency, built to run unimpeded from hunger and thirst. Instead, each night they soak in a tub of liquid, absorbing it through their thin skin. This liquid provides them with the nutrients they need."

I felt my stomach rumble and my head had begun to throb hours ago. I did not want to be disrespectful, but I was beginning to tire.

"I don't need to know the entire history of the universe. I am interested in what role humans have played," I said carefully.

The aliens glanced at each other, and again their muscles rippled.

"Your role? Your role is hardly significant."

My escort, who had thus far been fairly silent, aimed his thoughts in my direction.

"Humans have done more harm than good since they developed nuclear weapons. But you needn't worry about it."

The other alien spoke up. "That is beyond your concern now. To answer your earlier question, we are trying to give you an idea of how species all over the universe have evolved. May I continue?"

"Yeah, but...I'm kind of embarrassed here...I haven't eaten in a long time . . ."

One of the aliens pointed casually at the table; beneath his finger appeared a red piece of gummy candy. He flicked it towards me with his finger.

"Eat this. It will give you the nutrients you need for the next three days."

"I popped it in my mouth without question. It was sweet, and dissolved quickly on my tongue. Minutes later, my hunger was gone.

"Life evolved on a planet in your own galaxy. The race of people known as Hindus called them Deva. Due to their unique body chemistry, they have skin of gold and blue. Their eyes slant like those of Earthlings from the eastern hemisphere, except they are longer than those of a human; they look similar to the statues of Akhenaten."

I couldn't believe how satisfied I felt, sitting among these beings, whose names had not even been offered yet. I felt as if I was among wise uncles.

"How did you get here?" I asked, my curiosity too much to bear.

"In order for different species to travel from galaxy to galaxy and solar system to solar system, they built large, ring-shaped machines. One of your physicists, Michio Kaku, designed such a machine, and worked out all the math and how it would operate. Unfortunately, it took a type "three" civilization to build it, and he was not capable of the task. These machines bent space-time, allowing occupants to travel a large distance in a short time. You have certainly heard of a wormhole?"

"How could the spaceships possibly enter the worm-holes?"

"Nano-bots. They disassemble everything, and then reassemble them on the other side."

“This is how you get around the light speed limit,” I said thoughtfully.

“Precisely. The rings cannot be placed in random areas of the universe because of the nature of space-time, which is far too complex for us to explain right now. Instead, we place them in critical areas."

"Can anyone pass through a wormhole, or is it regulated?"

"Not everyone has access to the wormholes. That would invite catastrophe. But those who do must still request permission from the regulating board. There are many controls set to discourage such single-minded behavior."

I suddenly remembered a comment that Azazel had made about the extinction of the dinosaurs.

"Were you around for the extinction of the dinosaurs?" I asked.

My escort grew quiet, as if contemplating an answer. Then he flicked his hand and a monitor popped on across the room. It showed a dinosaur walking in a forest.

“This is Troodon. The Anunnaki mixed their DNA with this creature approximately seventy-five million years ago. Their descendants are the reptilians that do not have scaly skin. You can call them Hor, which is short for Homo reptilian. The Anunnaki took Hor off-world, and in time, this new species became too intelligent to control. Some of them escaped, returned to Earth, and made a life for themselves. The Deva—the lotus petal-eyed humans—protected Hor and agreed that Earth would belong to them. The Anunnaki, who believed themselves to be in control, devised a plan to destroy Hor. With advanced technology the Anunnaki guided an asteroid to hit Earth, so that the Deva would not suspect they had violated intergalactic law.”

“So there is an intergalactic law? I thought that was just a thing of fiction.”

“Even advanced civilizations require rules."

"So, were the Hor destroyed?"

"No. Even with their limited technology, they were still able to track the asteroid and retreated into underground caverns. Many of them survived and remained underground so that the Anunnaki would think they were dead.

"Did we originate from these beings?"

The alien seemed to consider something, and then thought better of it.

"About forty-six million years ago Architectus, now a light being, came to Earth and created a white man. Your story in Genesis relies on this event. He was not the first white man. Legend has it he was made in such a way that he lived for millions of years."

"So we are descended from that 'white man?'"

"Do not get ahead of me. There is much more to your history than one event."

I nodded an apology and beckoned the alien to continue.

"One hundred and sixty thousand years ago the Anunnaki had a war among themselves. Queen Tiamat, who is a character in the great book *Enuma Elish*, forced the Anunnaki to work. The Anunnaki were displeased with the new dictatorship and asked Ea to do something. Ea sent his son Marduk to defeat her.”

“Are you saying the characters in *Enuma Elish* are real?”

“Not exactly, but some of the story is based on real events and people. Tiamat made snake-men, according to *Enuma Elish*, to be her warriors. Marduk used advanced weaponry to defeat Tiamat.”

“I know *Enuma Elish*. It says Marduk used some sort of net so that none of her body parts or blood would escape. As if they didn’t want her to return.”

“Yes, if they had any part of her they could clone her. Marduk used his DNA and mixed it with early man and created the modern human.”

It took me a moment to catch up to the comment; it was a casual, almost nonchalant revelation.

"Are you saying that we're all part alien?”

“Yes, but you would have ended up looking the way you do regardless. DNA is DNA. Marduk simply sped up the process for you. The Anunnaki then turned humans into slaves. Other species followed suit. The Neanderthal man and the three-foot Homo Floresiensis were two examples of hybrids created by ETs. The Anunnaki commanded modern man to kill off Neanderthal because they were seen as a failed species."

"That sounds familiar. The Mayan creation myth speaks of two failed attempts to create man."

"Sometimes myth is based around real events. Around fifty thousand years ago, the Deva slept with Mongolians and the result was some of the families in India and Asia. To this day, they have legends about people from the sky coming down and mating with them. The Brahman, too, claim to be the offspring of the Deva Indra and the human Kunti."

My decline was sudden. I started getting very sleepy. I attributed it to the sheer volume of information. Yet, there was more to hear, so I tried to pay attention.

"Around twelve thousand years ago the Deva mixed with another group of humans and they migrated to Egypt. It was at this time that the Deva destroyed the Atlantis project started by the Anunnaki. The Deva were fed up with Anunnaki manipulating humans to be their slaves. Despite this destruction, the extraterrestrials continued to interact with man and use them. Many of your mythological stories are based on these interactions."

"We continued the trend of slavery . . . our past is not perfect either."

"Yes. It seems that all civilizations must torment others to prove their own worth—at least until their slaves fight back."

"It's a classic theme here on Earth," I announced. "The bully syndrome. Governments do it as much as school-kids."

The two aliens seemed to probe my thoughts. *What had I done?*

"It is this insight that keeps us interested in your species," my escort stated. "You seem to realize your predicament, but can do nothing to stop it."

I nodded in agreement. "We are taught that the good of the many outweighs that of individual freedoms."

There was a short pause, as if the aliens were considering what I said. Then the leader nodded, and I felt the attention focus back to the ancient stories.

"The Anunnaki helped the Egyptians build the Great Pyramid and other structures around the world. They mated with the Egyptians and made their offspring Pharaohs."

"So that is why the Egyptians claimed their Pharaohs were descended from the gods."

"Yes. One of the extraterrestrials fell in love with an Egyptian woman. In mythology, he is known as Ra. One day the woman asked Ra about the origins of man, and Ra loved her too much to lie to her. Ra went before the council and asked for permission to tell his wife about the origin of humans. They feared she would tell others, but Rah talked the council into forming a secret society. Only those people who belonged to the secret society—which would include Ra's children—would know the truth, that extraterrestrials created the human race."

"Why are you telling me this, then? My parents are from California."

"Eventually everyone must know. We have been working for centuries to pass the truth to the human race, one or two people at a time. It is much easier to convince one than hundreds."

"Aren't you afraid that there will be a religious war? You have admitted that you aren't gods."

"It is true that many humans will rebel against the idea of a mortal creator. But the time to announce the truth is still decades off."

"Will you be around to witness the announcement?"

There was a short pause. "Yes, in one form or another. "But it is not our job to get involved with such affairs. That is your job."

My heart leapt from my chest and I fell forward. As I fell to the floor, I saw it rush up to me. When I hit, my eyes snapped open, and I found myself at home in my own bed.

Chapter 6: Ancient Texts and Science

I spent a few days away from my computer after meeting with the dignitaries. I wasn't sure that it hadn't all been some kind of weird dream. But it didn't take long to rationalize that it had really happened. I sat down at my writing desk, trying to fight the urge to type. For a while, I kept myself busy traveling to the den and back, trading books from my large collection of ancient texts. I missed my alien friend. Azazel hadn't attempted to contact me since our "argument," and no one on Earth seemed to be riding the same wave of thought as me. I debated about forcing the issue, but finally decided to try to contact him. I organized everything on my desk a number of times before focusing on the ever-so-familiar drawing that I had named Azazel. For minutes, I stared, trying to beckon the figure to move. He wouldn't. My eyes burning with the effort, I closed them and dropped my head onto the desk.

A sudden noise startled me, and I snapped my head up, expecting to see my son. Instead, it was Azazel, approaching me dressed in all black.

“I must be dreaming again,” I said.

Azazel motioned for me to sit down on a silver chair. “You passed out at your desk.”

“That is becoming the norm,” I said, obliging him.

“Why do you spend so much time studying the ancient texts?” Azazel asked.

“I find it fascinating. Besides, they contain evidence that extraterrestrials visited Earth.”

“What kind of evidence, or proof? What texts are you speaking of?"

"The Bible, for one,” I said, forgetting for a moment that Azazel didn't necessarily know of the Bible. “People in biblical times seemed to know of scientific truths that their technology could not have predicted yet.”

Azazel rubbed his arm with a claw-like finger and prodded. "Go on . . ."

“I will. In Isaiah 42:*5*, the prophet talks about the heavens expanding. ". . . who created the heavens and expanded them out, who spread forth the Earth and what comes from it . . ." Isaiah mentions the heavens being expanded again in Chapter 45:*12*. Zechariah and Jeremiah also speak of the heavens expanding (Zechariah 12:*1*, Jeremiah 10:*12*). These passages hint of the Big Bang. Yet, the writings date to around 700BC, and oldest copies are contained in the Dead Sea scrolls dating from 300BC to 100AD. This was long before scientists had even given the Big Bang a name."

As an afterthought, I added a quick definition of the Big Bang. "It's not an explosion," I reiterated, "but a quick expansion, which is why these texts are so interesting."

Azazel’s stare could have burned a hole through me. “As if I don’t know of the Ultimate Expansion. Are these not references from the same "bible" that mentions a talking donkey?”

I chuckled. “Yes. Why would they stop telling their mythological stories just because extraterrestrials visited them? They just added to that their experiences with ETs.”

“But your thinking is flawed. You are reading these verses from the viewpoint of a human living in the 21st century. Before you primitive humans stumbled across the concept of the Big Bang, you did not interpret these verses the way you do now. Rather, through reading these verses, humans seemed to believe that "the heaven" was stretched out like a canopy above the Earth. Genesis Chapter One speaks of how the birds fly in the expanse of the heaven and how the stars were placed in the expanse of the heaven. That implies that these primitives believed the stars were only as high as the birds could fly.”

“That is possible, but if I'm not mistaken, the Bible says the "heavens" were expanded, not the “heaven.” The Hebrew grammar tells us that the word is plural; that is why the translators translated the phrase as "heavens." Perhaps the extraterrestrials told the prophets that the universe had expanded and was still expanding, and the prophets didn’t understand what that meant. Remember, the people back then believed that Earth was like an upside down bowl. They didn't believe there was a sky on the underside of the earth. That would explain why they talked about the heavens expanding and not the heaven expanding."

Azazel tapped his foot on the floor as if in thought. "And who is supposed to believe this theory that extraterrestrials somehow taught mankind about the universe?" he asked, the lines around his` mouth drawn up in a sly smile.

"You're right. By itself, it is not very convincing, but there are millions who will believe, simply because it is in the Bible. In Isaiah 40:*22* it says, 'It is he that sits upon the circuit of the earth . . .' The Hebrew word *chug* does not mean sphere, although ancient Rabbis had described the earth that way and used this verse as their reference. However, they learned from the Greeks that the Earth was a sphere."

Azazel stood up, moved his arm is a half circle, and said, "Come, let's walk. We need to speak of the significance of this fact. So, the Greeks knew the Earth was a sphere in 300BC. How is this meaningful?"

"Okay, the word *chug* means "circuit." Anyone can verify that by checking a Hebrew dictionary or Concordance. We call the circuit of the earth its orbit. *Chug* cannot mean the earth is a sphere, because the word order is wrong."

"And why would Jehovah be sitting on Earth's orbit? Is an orbit something you can sit on?"

"Well, again, they mixed their mythology with the extraterrestrial visitations. But look at Job 26:*7*. 'He stretches out the north over the empty place, and hangs the earth upon nothing.' He said this back in the days when people believed the Earth was being carried on an elephant's back."

"That's a much better reference, but it says he stretched out the north over the empty place. That is a primitive view, and is most likely what the prophets were talking about when they said he expanded the heavens. The north, south, east, and west heavens, which explains the plural heavens."

"Good point. But what about Genesis 1:*9-10*? It says that dry land rose above the water. The Hebrew *yabashah*, which means dry land, is in the singular. If it were talking about more than one land mass, it would say *yabashot*. Perhaps extraterrestrials gave them the knowledge of Pangaea. Genesis 10:*25* says the earth, which is the dry land, was divided. Now, of course the time-line is wrong, but the idea is there."

"I never learned Hebrew, but you make a strong case. You are saying that ETs taught humans how the Earth at one time was one land mass and slowly separated into continents. Of course, the author was more than likely referring to the division of people, because this chapter is talking about how Jehovah separated them by giving them different languages."

I looked up and found that we were no longer in my two-bedroom ranch home, but walking on a busy city street. Crossing a busy intersection, I hear Azazel's footfall, smooth yet somehow metallic. Around us, streaming chaotic lines of dream-people going about their daily lives seemed all too real, but I in the back of my mind I felt the contrary quiet of my own home. I continued our conversation, thoroughly enmeshed in the discussion.

"I don't know if you've studied Hinduism at all, but the *Srimad Bhagavatam*, a holy book written around 1000BC, mentions extraterrestrials directly. In Srimad Bhagavatam 5:*20:40* the book uses this phrase: '. . . to benefit all living beings in all the varied planets.' All living beings in all the varied planets is no doubt a reference to life forms living on other planets." I said. My eyes drifted across the street to a beautiful woman in the process of feeding her parking meter.

"She's not real," Azazel announced.

"Yeah I know, but she is pretty."

"Humans and their hormones. It is amazing to me that your species has evolved this far with such a barbaric emotional foundation."

"Our 'barbaric' emotions include sacrifice, honor, compassion, love...I could continue..."

"No need to. Continue with your train of thought. I am familiar with Hinduism, yet I don't know much of the role science plays in their ancient texts."

I grabbed a book from a shelf that suddenly appeared in front of me. On a busy city street, this was no small accomplishment. "I am going to quote the next reference exactly as it appears in the *Srimad Bhagavatam.*

5:22:2. 'Śrī Śukadeva Gosvāmī clearly answered: When a potter's wheel is moving and small ants located on that big wheel are moving with it, one can see that their motion is different from that of the wheel because they appear sometimes on one part of the wheel and sometimes on another. Similarly, the signs and constellations, with Sumeru and Dhruvaloka on their right, move with the wheel of time, and the antlike sun and other planets move with them. The sun and planets, however, are seen in different signs and constellations at different times. This indicates that their motion is different from that of the zodiac and the wheel of time itself.'

"This description of a galaxy is amazing for its time, because back then no one knew what a galaxy looked liked. No one even imagined a galaxy to be disc-shaped, yet this verse described all the stars and planets rotating around a center point, liking it to a potter's wheel."

I flipped through the book a little, pulling up another page in the text.

"Look here, at verse 5:*23:2*. It states:

'Established by the supreme will of the Supreme Personality of Godhead, the polestar, which is the planet of Mahārāja Dhruva, constantly shines as the central pivot for all the stars and planets. The unsleeping, invisible, most powerful time factor causes these luminaries to revolve around the polestar without cessation.'

"Dhruva Maharaja is a spirit. The polestar, which is the center of the galaxy, is his planet. Notice it says that the polestar shines, and it is true the center of most galaxies shine; they look like large suns. The Hindus also believe there is a spirit that lives in our sun. Again, this seems to be mythology mixing with what the ETs taught them."

I paused to see if Azazel had anything to interject. As the dignitaries had been, he appeared stoic, if a little amused at our walk through downtown New York City.

"Why New York?" I asked. "Why not a quiet country road?"

Azazel shrugged, as much as his thin shoulders allowed, anyway. "A country road doesn't have your favorite roadside food."

I chuckled, startled by the down-to-Earth tone in his voice.

"Thanks, thanks a lot."

My mind edged itself back to the discussion at hand, and I remembered the book in my hands, now suddenly at the last passage I wanted to read from.

"See what you think of this verse," I said, clearing my voice to read.

5:23:3 says, 'When bulls are yoked together and tied to a central post to thresh rice, they tread around that pivot without deviating from their proper positions—one bull being closest to the post, another in the middle, and a third on the outside. Similarly, all the planets and all the hundreds and thousands of stars revolve around the polestar, the planet of Mahārāja Dhruva, in their respective orbits, some higher and some lower. Fastened by the Supreme Personality of Godhead to the machine of material nature according to the results of their fruitive acts, they are driven around the polestar by the wind and will continue to be so until the end of creation. These planets float in the air within the vast sky, just as clouds with hundreds of tons of water float in the air or as the great śyena eagles, due to the results of past activities, fly high in the sky and have no chance of falling to the ground.'

Azazel's eyes lit up. "That is a very enlightened view of the universe, considering the times. I should read this book. It is interesting, as it is true that some planets are higher or lower in the galaxy."

"Yes. But what is interesting about these passages is that the author claims to get the information from beings that live on other planets."

We crossed a busy intersection that only exists in my dream world. Streaming chaotic lines of dream-people going about their daily lives seemed all too real, but I knew I was dreaming.

We sat down at a small round table outside of a sidewalk cafe. A cute waitress dressed in a white uniform sauntered up beside me.

"What would you like?" she asked casually.

"I'll take a chocolate mocha with marshmallows on top," I ordered.

Azazel cocked his head sideways as a dog does when he hears a strange sound.

"What?"

"You know the coffee isn't real, don't you?"

"Yes, I know that nothing here is real, but my taste buds don't need to know that. Besides, I can't drink coffee in real life."

"I see. Do you have any more passages that might be interesting to me?"

My hand flipped the worn pages of the *Srimad Bhagavatam*, traveling without my conscious awareness. They stopped at Verse 3:*11:2*.

'Atoms are the ultimate state of the manifest universe. When they stay in their own forms without forming different bodies, they are called the unlimited oneness. There are certainly different bodies in physical forms, but the atoms themselves form the complete manifestation.'

Although the translation uses the word atoms, literally it would be translated as "the ultimate small particle."

"I am starting to understand why you enjoy studying ancient texts," Azazel said with a sigh.

"But wait," I interrupted. "The next verses talk about how to measure atomic time. This is a subject that modern science is only now beginning to discover, yet this book is talking about it as if it is the simplest concept."

The pretty waitress returned with my mocha. I thanked her and took a sip. It was creamy and chocolaty, just as I had remembered.

"Most fascinating," Azazel stated, a little late.

"Yes, it is. I mean what are the chances that the ancient Hindus would think up the idea of atomic time?"

Azazel chuckled quietly. "No, I mean, it is most fascinating that you are actually enjoying your mocha as if it were real."

"Well, it tastes real enough."

"I suppose so. And yes, it is very unlikely ancient Hindus thought up the ideas you have mentioned without the help of a more advanced intelligence."

"Well, the Hindus themselves claim that extraterrestrials taught them this stuff. Of course, this particular book has many far-fetched stories as well. Many that have to be fiction. It's that contrast in the book between myth and accurate knowledge beyond their time that makes it so compelling to read. You can tell by reading the myths in the book that these Hindu writers were not the most intelligent in the village, yet when they share the information they claim was taught to them by ETs, they sound as sharp as a razor."

Azazel stood up. "The most impressive thing about some of the information we find in this book is that a lot of it went against the folk beliefs of their culture."

Azazel attempted again to shrug. "That makes a good argument for there being some kind of outside influence, then, doesn't it?"

I nodded. Azazel stretched and took a step backwards. An oval portal appeared behind him.

"I have had a wonderful discussion with you this evening. I am sure that if we had more time to converse, we would discover many more interesting topics. However, I have to return to my own circumstances now. Please forgive me."

Azazel stepped abruptly through the portal, and a flash of lightning exploded in front of my eyes. I clenched my eyes shut briefly. Upon opening them, I found myself once again sitting at my computer desk. Though my head hurt and I was sweating terribly, I couldn't help but smile. I felt for the first time that *he* had been enlightened by *my* words.

Chapter 7: Bible, UFOs, and Extraterrestrials

The next few nights were strangely Azazel-free. I sat at the computer after dinner each night, stared at the picture for a while, and then wrote until the words on the screen began to blur in my head.

Tonight, I wrote until a bit after midnight and decided to turn in, still no word from my alien friend.

I was in the land between awake and sleep when I felt the familiar presence sneak behind me.

“You think you can just invade my dreams whenever you feel like it?” I said, not too unkindly.

“Would you prefer me not to?”

I thought. A part of me wanted to say yes, simply because I wouldn't have to worry about whether I was losing my mind.

“No, I like your visitations.”

“Last time we talked, you had shown me compelling examples of ancient people learning science from extraterrestrials. Although at the time I was not familiar with the Hindu texts, I have been studying them. I have also studied the Bible and consulted my historians about some of the stories. You may not want to know this, but the story of Adam and the first human Marduk made reflects the same historical event.”

“Does that mean that our biblical Adam never existed?”

Azazel pinched his long fingers against his chin, a signature that I had come to recognize as a sign that he was trying to simplify his thoughts.

“Yes and no. The story of Adam does mimic a historical event. Remember when you visited the dignitaries and they told you about an Anunnaki that built a human from the curve of his blood?”

“Yeah. The story of Marduk in *Enuma Elish*,” I said.

“Correct. Marduk took the curve of his blood and mixed it with a primate and made a slave race. The story of Elohim the Anunnaki making Adam is a modified version of the same historical event. In the Bible it says in Genesis 9:*4* that you shall not eat the flesh with its life—that is—its blood.”

“The life in the blood is the DNA?” I asked.

“In Genesis 2 it says that Elohim took one of the curves of Adam and made woman. I know you know Hebrew and are aware that the Hebrew word translated as rib means “curve” or “side.” When it says Elohim caused a deep sleep to fall upon Adam and he slept, he was actually put under anesthesia.”

“But according to the Bible they are not a slave race.”

“In the Bible they are called "the slaves of Jehovah." One of the names of Jehovah is *Qana*, and as you know, that means "jealous." Jehovah told Adam not to eat of the Tree of the Knowledge of Good and Evil, or that day he would die. The Nachash told Eve that she would not actually die if she ate of the tree, and when she did eat, she did not die. Later on Jehovah says they have become like "one of us" to know good and evil. To prevent them from living too long, Jehovah sent angels to guard the Tree of Life. The Anunnaki were afraid of humans becoming too knowledgeable. If they became too knowledgeable they would not make good slaves.”

I scratched my head. I grew up believing that Adam and Eve were the first humans, and although I had long done away with that belief, I still wanted to believe that Jehovah was the spiritual entity that had made Adam. I asked Azazel, "What did the Tree of Life represent?"

"The Tree of Life did not represent anything. It was how the Hebrews changed the historical story. The secret to the long life of the Anunnaki was a drink created by their scientists. They took it with them wherever they went. The Anunnaki that remained on Earth to watch over the humans didn't want the humans to discover this drink."

"This is according to your historians. Do you believe them?"

"They have no reason to lie," Azazel said quickly.

"How do I know you are not lying?" I snapped back.

"I have no reason to lie."

I sat back and sighed.

"Perhaps you're right. Hey, let's go to a store with fresh-baked cookies and pie," I said, with a smile as big as the crescent moon that shone down on us.

"Cake and pie—that's all you can think about as I share this knowledge with you?"

"Well, I can't eat it in real life. Besides, I can eat and listen at the same time."

"A multi-tasking genius," he said.

"Your human side must be possessing you, because that was a hint of genuine sarcasm."

"I must be spending too much time with you," Azazel said.

"Must be."

A scent of fresh-baked cookies and pie led me to a small shop that would make anyone's grandma jealous. Oil lamps and candles lit the small shop. I ordered oatmeal cookies and a hot German apple pie.

I dipped my fork into the apple pie and said to Azazel, "Here, try some."

"I don't think I would care much for human food."

"You're half human, right? Just try it."

"But, it's not real."

I waved the piece of pie attached to my fork in front of his face, "Can you smell it?"

He cocked his head back, lifted his nose and inhaled. With a slight grin on his face he said, "Yes, I smell it."

"Then it's real enough."

I pushed the piece of pie towards his mouth; he hesitated, then quickly snatched it off my fork and placed it in his mouth.

"What do you think?"

"It's good. It's actually good."

"See, I told you," I said with confidence.

Azazel ordered his own pie and we ate together as he continued to share his knowledge with me.

"You remember the story in Exodus, Chapter three?"

"Yes, the burning bush," I said, after a small hesitation.

"Correct. Moses saw a burning bush that was not consumed, and he went to get a closer look. Before he could discover that it was a hologram, a voice boomed from a megaphone and told him not to come any closer because the place he stood on was Holy ground."

"That's not how the story goes."

"I know. Ra, who is one of the Anunnaki, is whom Moses served while in Egypt. Ra didn't want Moses to know that he was using hologram technology to cause the bush illusion. The Anunnaki liked that humans believe them to be gods or angels."

"They must have big egos."

"You could put it that way. Humans are more likely to obey angels or gods than they are to obey extraterrestrials from outer space."

"True."

I replaced my old image of the burning bush with a newer version, imagining Ra's right-hand man telling him to get Moses' attention. I watched in my mind Ra placing a hologram of a burning bush in a cleft of rocks. Moses saw the light and went to check it out. In my mind, the characters began to speak.

"He is getting too close, Ra! He's going to discover it's not real. Do something!" Ra adjusted his voice with the advanced technology to make it boom through the sky and said, "Don't come any closer!"

Moses stopped, scared of the loud voice, but his curiosity got the best of him and he blurted out, "Why?"

I imagined Ra then deciding to tell Moses that the ground was holy, even demanding that he take his shoes off.

Azazel smiled, clearly following the thoughts that I had just had.

"Yes. It happened somewhat like that. Now, on to other things. I have noticed lately that you have been studying 2nd Samuel 22:*10*."

"Yeah, I've been trying to figure out what it means. It mentions that 'he bowed the heavens' and came down; thick darkness was under his feet. He rode 'on a cherub, and flew;' 'he was seen upon the wings of the wind' making darkness around him a canopy, thick clouds, a gathering of water."

"This verse refers to one of the Anunnaki spacecraft that is capable of bending space time. It makes a wormhole that allows you to travel from one side of the galaxy to the other in a few hours."

"Ah, he bowed the heavens. He bent space-time. Brilliant!" I said.

I finished my apple pie and bit into my warm oatmeal cookie. Azazel must have seen the pleasure on my face. He reached for one of my cookies. I put my hands over them, "Hey, they're not real, remember?"

Azazel squinted and tilted his head.

I bellowed. "I'm just kidding! Try one, they are great."

Azazel took a cookie and unceremoniously began chewing on it.

"This same craft is mentioned in Ezekiel Chapter One and Chapter Ten, and it is also referred to as a cherub. This is the "cherub" that Jehovah flies in. The wheels within a wheel are gyroscope-looking devices that produce enough gravity to bend space-time. At the end of Chapter One, a glass dome opens up and a human-looking figure dressed in metal steps out of his chair.

"Remember, in the book of Kings, Elijah it taken up by a whirlwind into a spinning, burning chariot. If you imagine a spinning, burning chariot, car, or even shoebox, it looks like an orange-colored flying saucer."

"Are you saying that Elijah was abducted?"

"I am saying that the story was based on a person that was abducted."

"I see," I responded, gazing out the cafe window. "Actually, now that I think about it, in Zechariah Chapter Five it says Zechariah sees a large flying scroll. That is bizarre. It is like seeing a large book flapping in the sky."

"What is important in this story is that Zechariah was able to identify the flying object, even though it was not a normal object to see flying in the sky. If Zechariah could identify a flying scroll, should he also be able to identify a flying talent?"

"Yes, he should—ah, and later in the story the angel said, 'Look up, what do you see?' Zechariah said he didn't know."

"Precisely, Azazel said. "He didn't know, yet it says they were flying talents. And talents are coins, which are similar to disk shapes, yet they were not talents because the angel said they 'resembled' talents. Flying saucers resemble talents."

"I have read and studied Zechariah so many times. I can't believe this never crossed my mind. This is amazing! The angel showed Zechariah the future, and in the future, he saw flying objects that resembled flying coins. And in the next chapter, he saw two metal mountains floating in the sky and chariots came out from between them. That could be smaller ships coming out of a larger ship."

"Exactly!"

"What about the star that the wise men followed until it stood over Jesus?" I pondered. "Stars don't move, and then stand still. They might appear to move, but they do not appear to stand still. Not unless the Earth stops rotating."

"My historians did not tell me about that, but they could have been following a spacecraft, because when a spacecraft is high enough it resembles a star."

"Right, and Revelation Chapter Nine comes to mind. I have always wondered what John saw. It says he saw locusts with metal breast plates and tails of scorpions with fire coming from their mouths."

"Imagine a modern space craft that resembles a helicopter. It shoots fire out of its mouth, so the guns might be mounted in the front?"

"Is that possible?" I wondered aloud. "Was John a contactee?"

"My historians did not enlighten me about that."

"John talks about Abbadon coming out of a bottomless pit. I have often wondered about that."

"A wormhole, or black hole," Azazel offered.

"True!" I said. "Yeah, a wormhole is a pit and it is bottomless."

"If John was a contactee, perhaps they told him about the wormhole technology. We have wormhole machines situated around space that bend space time, allowing us to travel a long distance in a short amount of time, without going faster than the speed of light."

"Like star gates, as in the TV show Stargate SG-1?"

"Something like that, if it's the show that I read about in *Popular Earth Sci-Fi* a few nights ago."

I couldn't help but chuckle at his words. "What, are you telling me that you have a magazine that covers our television shows?"

Azazel stood back on his heels and gave me a strange look before answering.

"Well, actually, it's more like a guide, so that we are aware of your species' sentiments."

He was so serious; I sucked in the last chuckle and straightened my mouth.

"That means that Abbadon is the extraterrestrial that is going to open a wormhole close to Earth, which would allow an army to come through. One could interpret the army in Revelation Nine as extraterrestrial," I said.

"Yes, but if that is the case, and I cannot elaborate any more, then Abbadon will need the pass code to open it."

Azazel's demeanor changed quickly after that, and a quiet minute later, he quickly stated that he had to go. Before I had a chance to ask him about it any further, he was gone, leaving me alone in my mind. I snapped awake, then drifted back to sleep thinking about Armageddon and the secrets of the Bible.

Chapter 8: Origin of Mythology

I stayed up late last night. Since Azazel had left me so quickly after our last meeting, I'd been thinking about what he didn't want to tell me. Was he bound by a secret that was larger than us both, or had he just allowed his humanity and its flaws to get the better of him?

I sat at my spot, this time with no computer or typewriter available—one had crashed, the other had a sticky key that made it impossible to write a complete sentence. Instead, I had a pen and a pad of paper, with notes and doodles already scribbled down the margins. As I sat there ready to write, it was as if on cue; sleep seized me like a drug.

He showed up right on time.

“All primitive humanoids on varied planets have developed religion for the same reasons,” Azazel said, apparently out of the blue.

“Is this how Halflings do things?" I said. "They make you fall asleep so they can pop some idea into your head that comes out of nowhere? Do you like dream walking that much?”

Azazel seemed taken aback. “You were tired. Would you rather me not have caused you to sleep?”

"No, I appreciate that part."

But it was not all right, I thought. If Halflings could dream walk, what could their full-blooded fathers do?

Azazel read my mind. "I do not like the term ‘Halfling.’ It conjures a much too primitive image."

"I'm sorry," I said, still distracted enough to ignore the insult in his voice.

"I came to apologize for my abrupt departure. And to explain some of the mysteries of the world."

I nodded.

"But I cannot share everything I know. It is against the oath I swore to the Elders."

Again, I nodded. It had been a jarring few months. One minute I was awake and the next I was dreaming about having conversations with an alien. My sense of reality still refused to believe that he was real.

I spoke simply to clear my mind.

“You said something about humanoids all developing religion for the same reason?”

Azazel bobbed his large head up and down.

“Similar reasons, yes. Tell me, what were the first drawings on Earth?”

“Cave drawings, I believe.”

“Yes, but what were they of?”

I tried to think, but the stark landscape Azazel had brought along with him in this dream seemed too cold and in-humane.

“Animals and humans," I answered. As I waited for him to absorb and respond, I decided to change the backdrop of this dream. I imagined winding trees, some flowers, and waterfalls.

“You've created a beautiful setting," Azazel said. "Quite different from your normal choice.”

“Yeah,” I answered. I held my finger out and an exotic butterfly landed on it. “I’m in a Japanese garden mood, I guess.”

Azazel paused to reflect. “I suppose so. Let's finish our talk so that you might enjoy the setting in peace."

"Sure thing," I said. "You were talking about cave drawings..."

"Yes," Azazel said. “The oldest evidence of worship on Earth is the worship of animals and ancestors, right?”

I nodded.

“This happens on every planet that has intelligent life. Eventually the new intelligent life form ponders where it came from. The parents tell their children: 'You came from us.' Of course, the next question is: 'Where did you come from?' and the answer is 'From our parents.'

"I see."

"To help with the grieving process, life forms create an afterworld for their loved ones, including their parents. Since they believe that their parents live on after they die, they believe that the ghosts of their ancestors must still be around. They tell each other ghost stories and give them powers. They tell their kids, 'If you do them wrong they might harm you.'"

“So, they pray to their ancestors out of fear?”

“Not just 'they.' You as well. But they don't pray just out of fear; they also pray out of respect. They did love them, after all. They believe that their ancestors can help them in times of trouble.”

“Going back to my ancestors--the cave drawers; worshiping the ghosts of ancestors would seem to answer any questions about what happens after death, but what of the question of where Life originated?"

"It was only natural that they believed life originated from Earth. Simple observation led them to believe all life comes from the Earth. After all, Earth grew forth the plants. But that was not the only reason they called the Earth 'Mother.' They also thought of the Earth as mother because women mammals produced food to sustain life; similarly, the Earth produced food for all of Her children."

I tried to gather my reaction. "So, out of fear that Mother would stop growing plants, they worshipped her. They asked her to continue providing food for them."

"Precisely. Worshiping the Earth made sense in those times. They added a Father (the sky) to accompany the female Earth. The sky or the sun became Father, because plants did not grow without the sun. Furthermore, the plants needed rain to survive, and rain came from the sky."

"But why did the sky have to be Father?" I interrupted.

"Simple observation. Men put their 'seed' into women, and she produced life; so too, the sky rained its 'seed' onto the Earth, and she produced life."

"That makes sense."

"Indeed, the worship of nature made sense then. As humans evolved, they questioned. 'Why does Father leave us each night, and return in the morning?'"

"If the Sun is Father, and Earth is Mother, then what is the moon?"

"Cute," Azazel said, sounding annoyed. "Can I continue?"

I nodded.

"Through years or generations, they came to the conclusion that the Father leaves each night for similar reasons fathers back then left each day: to hunt. If the Earth was Mother, and the Sun was Father, it only made sense that the Moon was Son."

"The first Trinity," I interjected again, though this time he didn't seem as unpleased.

"You could say that, although they didn't believe as Christians do, of the Father, Son and Holy Ghost all being One. What they DID believe continued to evolve. The moon ruled the night, while the father was gone; that meant that there were millions of other Fathers and Sons out there, one to represent each star or planet. These stars and planets, then, needed their own stories. Eventually, and for reasons that I won't get into this time, the art of Astrology and Numerology were born."

My mind reeled with all of the information. Sacred numbers, gods and the universe all jumbled into a whorl that threatened to take my breath.

Azazel continued. "Soon, humans did rituals to worship the gods as they aligned with other gods, that is, the stars and planets. Religion evolved out of these rituals. For instance most every ancient religion believed the number seven was sacred, because there were seven visible natural satellites: Sun, Moon, Mercury, Venus, Mars, Jupiter, and Saturn. That's why the Hebrews to this day balance their sins on Yom Kippur, in the month of Libra, the astrological sign of the scales."

A throbbing thunder blast through my head. The continuous stream of information and lack of sleep was getting to me. I heard myself speak, *that is my voice*, for I didn't know where the thoughts had come from.

"When the aliens came down to Earth, humans modified their gods to emulate the aliens; thus our gods turned into humanoids. A mixing of beliefs formed a new religion..."

I heard Azazel agree, and then something strange occurred. He began to disintegrate right in front of me. As dreams had a tendency to do, I found myself transported from Azazel's side in our Japanese garden to a completely unfamiliar grey-backed planet. I could breathe the air, but still stood breathless as a montage of images settled across my vision. I saw two grey-skinned aliens speaking in English, discussing their role as gods to the "primitive Earthlings."

"We can ask them to do anything, and they will do it willingly," one said.

The other chuckled. "They think we're gods. They will cook for us, feed us, fan us, and even have sex with us."

From there the pictures morphed one to another; in my heart I knew I was watching the history of mankind's religion, as worship moved from Earth and Sun to aliens to half-God, half-man; the images were out of focus, the voices distorted, and my head spun with it all. In the world of the living, I would have passed out; as it was, I could do nothing but let it all consume me.

Perhaps it was the brain's way of saving me from my own thoughts, perhaps it was something that had really happened, but at that point, a noise startled me awake. I was drenched in sweat, my fists clenched. Under the influence of fresh sleep, I gazed around. The way the light meandered through our dim hallway told me it was just before sunrise.

I went to sweep the paper and pen from my desk, and noticed that there were scribbles of symbols all over the page. Interested, but too tired to contemplate it now, I folded the paper and stuck it in my pocket. My head throbbed with the memory of the "dream" and all of its implications. I stood up on wobbly legs and made my way to the bedroom and plopped on my bed.

Chapter 9: ESS

I went on with my life after that day. That is, until the accident.

I was outside putting up our holiday lights when the ladder went out from under me and I careened to the ground. I felt a swift pain go through my body and then a fuzzy image appeared in the night.

"Azazel?" I mumbled, half-in and half-out of consciousness.

"It's getting dangerous for me."

His voice was strained.

"Why?"

He grabbed me right off of the ground. I looked back and caught a glimpse of my body.

"I have shared information with you that I was not supposed to share," Azazel said.

"Am I dead?" I asked.

I did not receive an immediate response.

"I have more I must share," he said instead. "About Moses."

"Sure," I answered. "Am I dead, though?"

Azazel shook his head. "Is that all you can think about?!"

"Well, yeah!" I blurted. "It's kind of a big thing for humans."

"No, you're not dead. Now, onto the story. I don't have much time!"

I didn't even have time to change the dreamscape this time. He simply dragged me along behind him, as if he were running for his life. His speech was quick, and edgy.

"The story of Moses is based on a real person. He was raised in Egypt, as the story in the Bible says. Moses, like the rest of the people in the house of Pharaoh, would have grown up learning Egyptian magic. He would have worshipped the gods of Egypt, including Ra."

Slowly I saw the backdrop of the dream change to reflect his words. The deserts of Egypt, along with a number of small huts, popped up behind Azazel.

"Moses learned the origin of man that was taught by the Egyptian Secret Society, or ESS. These people had plans to control the country, but the Hebrews rebelled against them, refusing to accept the gods of Egypt as their own."

I could smell the dry air of the desert. It was as if the setting was becoming more real with time.

Azazel continued talking in a hurried fashion, looking every so often behind us.

"The Egyptians tried to mix with the Hebrews in order to persuade them to worship Ra, but they would not. Moses, who was a master magician in Egypt due to his upbringing in the house of Pharaoh, was sent to infiltrate the Hebrews and persuade them to worship Ra."

"So, Moses was raised in Pharaoh's house?"

The powers answered my question almost immediately. In front of me, a river appeared, deep and cool to the touch. The smell of it filled the air.

As I watched, a basket appeared, and without being told, I knew that the baby was Moses.

"One of the Anunnaki came to the family of Moses and told his mother to put Moses in a basket and place him in the river," Azazel explained.

"The daughter of Pharaoh went to the river as commanded by her father and she found baby Moses. The house of Pharaoh raised him to worship Ra."

I felt my legs tiring, even in this dream setting, as Azazel whisked me from one setting to another. The dreamscape reflected the fear he must have felt as he ran from whatever powers he'd gone against.

"In his 30s, Moses killed an Egyptian and fled Egypt with the house of Pharaoh threatening his life. This was an illusion. Moses then met a follower of Jehovah named Jethro. He pretended to convert. Then, using ESS magic, he convinced the Hebrews that Jehovah worked miracles through him."

"Where is this going?" I asked, wondering if perhaps Azazel was losing track of his own story.

"Moses gained the trust of the Hebrews through magic and lies. He soon had them murdering for Jehovah, slaughtering whole nations in His name. But the 'Jehovah' Moses served was Ra."

"That can't be right. Ra and Jehovah cannot be one and the same."

Azazel grew impatient.

"The Jehovah that Moses served was Ra. Ra's symbol was the sun, and so was Moses' Jehovah. Psalms 84*:11* calls Jehovah 'the sun.' A prophecy in Malachi says the 'sun' of righteousness will come. And Moses sang a song in which he clearly denotes Jehovah as the sun."

"Where?"

"Deuteronomy 33*:26-27*. . . . 'Who rides upon the sky in your help, and in his excellency on the sky. The east is his dwelling, and underneath are the ancient arms.'"

Even in this hurried place, I could remember the verse as I studied it in Hebrew.

"I always wondered what *meona elohey qedem* meant. *Qedem* means "origins" or "east." The sun rises in the east, and the east was important to Ra worship. The Hebrews had to face east when they prayed."

We stopped walking for a moment, Azazel beckoning me to sit.

"Think Judah 'the Lion,' he said. "In astrology, the Lion's planetary ruler is the Sun. And consider the etymology of the Hebrew in the Deuteronomy verse: *Meona* means 'resting.' *Elohey* means 'God of.' Together with *Qedem*, this phrase reads 'the resting place of the God of east.'"

I responded with a stout smile.

"In this context, it does sound like they're talking about the sun."

"Exactly," Azazel said, and glanced around as if he were being followed.

"But," I interjected. "That by itself is not enough proof that Moses secretly enticed the Hebrews to worship Ra."

"Have you no faith?" Azazel said.

"I'm not sure anymore."

"There is more evidence. Hebrews did not start calling Jehovah 'Yah' until after they left Egypt. Yah is the Egyptian word for moon—and Ea (pronounced yah) is a pagan deity of Sumer. Hebrews also did not begin to say amen after curses until after they left Egypt."

"You've lost me," I said.

Azazel beckoned me to be quiet and we started moving again.

"What are you running from?" I tried to ask. "Why can't we sit and talk?"

He dismissed me with a wave of his long fingers and began to count on them.

"One, an Egyptian will curse you in the name of a god, such as Amon (amen) or Ra. Two, the Egyptians had golden arks before the Hebrews made the Ark of the Covenant according to Moses' commands. Three, the Cherubs that Moses commanded be built resemble those found in Egypt. Finally, the Hebrews did not offer sacrifices of bread, wine, and other manners of food until after they left Egypt, where such offerings were common."

"So, you've proven that Moses influenced the Hebrews enough for them to take on many of the Egyptian ways of doing things. But does that make them followers of Ra?"

"In a roundabout way. Moses worshipped Ra, the Hebrews followed his teachings; therefore, they worshipped Ra."

A bright flash temporarily took my attention from my alien friend. When I looked back, he was gone. I screamed for him, but got no response. Blindly I ran into the darkness.

"Here, quickly!" his voice rang. I followed it and found myself in a crevice not much bigger than the size of a twin bed.

"What's going on?" I whispered.

"Interpret those symbols," he said.

"What symbols?" I said, too nervous to remain quiet.

He didn't answer. Instead, he stood and pushed me into the light. In my mind, I saw a piece of paper marked with inked symbols. It was familiar, but I couldn't quite recall how.

I wouldn't have time to contemplate it until two nights later when I awoke from what the doctors called a drug-induced coma. I couldn't remember what I'd done or where I had been during those two days of unconsciousness, but I felt an urgent need to find my alien research. I felt bad asking my wife to indulge my irrationality, but she didn't seem to mind, and as I looked through the papers later that night, it suddenly hit me.

"Where are the pants I had on?"

My wife snapped awake.

"Pants...?"

"The ones I had on when I fell . . ."

She leapt over to the small closet, opened it up and pulled out a plastic drawstring bag.

I almost yanked the pants from her hands. In the back pocket, the folded paper was damp, but otherwise unhurt. I gave my wife a quick peck on the cheek and unfolded the paper carefully.

It took a few moments for the symbols to kick in, but not as long as it might have if I'd been at home with access to the hundreds of books on the subject.

They were the symbols of the Jewish freemasonry, still in use by the Grand Lodge of the State of Israel. The eye of Ra was used as a symbol of the freemason, as well as serving as the eye of illumination on the U.S. dollar bill. Other symbols on the crest of the Grand Lodge were the Square, the Compass, the Christian Cross, the Jewish Star of David and the Muslim Crescent moon, all of which I had written on that piece of paper. Traditionally, only three symbols--the square, the compass, and the capital letter G, truly represented the Freemasons. The square stood for the master builder, the compass for the Sun, and the G for Gaia (a goddess of the Earth).

What did drawing the symbols have to do with Azazel and what had just happened? I couldn't have answered that in the hospital; what I imagined was frightening, and indicated that the ESS might still be a big player in the ways of the modern world and its many governments.

Chapter 10: Agendas

My recovery time was slow; at night I found it all but impossible to sit at the desk and concentrate on writing, much less try to initiate a meeting with a maybe-imaginary alien. However, it seemed destined to happen, and not through an accident this time. It was, in fact, the most realistic experience I had ever had with my friend.

I was in bed; my wife had taken my son to the store. Usually, she would have left him with me, but she must have felt sorry for my lapse in sanity.

It felt like an odd day as it was; the sun seemed to melt into the mountains and the sky was lined with orange and pink. I carefully made my way outside on the back deck, so I could enjoy the grandeur in relative peace.

At first I thought I was asleep, but the setting was so familiar and real; I could smell the remnants of last week's wildfire that had been doused as it neared the canyon.

Azazel walked up to me, but his movements were not fluid, and in his eyes I saw no sparkle of recognition.

"This is the last thing I will say," Azazel said.

"What do you mean?" I asked, sitting up stout in my seat.

"I haven't much time," he said. I could hear the whirr of electricity, as if a motor was running, and the sound plagued me, even as I attempted to focus on Azazel.

"Dragon Empire has an agenda for Earth. It wants to transform the planet into a Utopia using nano-bot technology that will clean Earth's air, water and soil of all pollution; it will cure every disease. These nano-bots will become the servants of man, building whatever their hearts desire."

I began to interrupt.

"In return," he continued, a little louder, "humans must search for the information on how to escape our ultra-galaxy before it collapses."

"The big crunch," I whispered, more to myself.

"Those who refuse to cooperate will be denied access to the nano-bots. They will continue to get sick, die of cancer and illness, while those who do as requested continue to live. The rebels will have no luxuries. In essence, those who help more receive more pleasures, including what only money can buy right now. But they must be fully dedicated to the cause."

Listening to him speak so clearly and bluntly scared me for the first time since we'd met. The implications of such a society were enormous.

Azazel's form wavered a bit, and I finally realized what had made that whirring sound. My friend was no more standing in front of me than he had been that first night, after I had finished that drawing. Through some kind of holographic technology, he was presenting me with a final message.

"Where are you at?" I asked, knowing that a hologram couldn't possibly respond to my questions.

But he did seem to respond, in a way. His voice got hushed, and he glanced behind him before starting again.

"Through organizations like the ESS, the Dragon Empire has kept men ignorant of their true potential. Society is set up to keep humans so busy that they don't have time for anything but basic societal survival. Human children spend their most creative years in school, spoon-fed what "society" needs them to know. After schooling is over, the simple task of raising a family is paramount, consuming all thought. What you refer to as "spare time" is spent in wasteful activity to cleanse the mind of hostility and aggravation. But what you humans do not do is find time to truly learn who you are, and what your true galactic potential is. You allow religion to tell you what is the truth, instead of finding it out for yourselves."

Suddenly, I felt very queasy. I had the feeling that what he would say next would be the most profound thought he had shared with me.

"I have learned a lot from you, my friend. I have learned that I love apple pie."

I had been holding my breath, and with that I nearly passed out as laughter streamed from my mouth.

He winked, and I felt in him a sincere human being. I missed him, his presence. I would miss it; I had a feeling, for the rest of my life.

"My time is nearly up," he said, an obvious segue back to the topic at hand.

"The Dragon Empire is on its way, and it does not look like they will be stopped."

Questions ran through my mind, of why this would happen with so many intelligent life forms out there.

"I know you must have many questions, but I cannot answer them all. I'm sorry."

"It's not your fault," I said to the hologram.

"To ease your mind, and assist in your spiritual healing, I will tell you that I have moved on to a better plane; a much nicer, more peaceful arena. Where I can enjoy my apple pie in peace."

My breath hitched with that revelation. Even as he had shown up in holographic form, I had believed that he was alive, hiding out from those who would keep him from speaking to me further. But now I realized that he was not simply hiding.

"They took my life, but they could not claim my soul," Azazel said in response.

"How is it that you seem to know what I am saying?" I asked, suddenly unsure that what I was looking at was a hologram.

"I am in the ghost world, the in-between for every humanoid after death. My dream-walking skills have served me well; but I do not have the strength to continue. I must go "into the light," as your movies so love to say."

"Wait!" I yelled, so much to say to him.

"I'm sorry," he whispered, his form flickering once, twice, and then disappearing completely.

I sat there in the now darkness, looking at the spot that he had disappeared from. Hoping, perhaps, that he would suddenly appear back. How long I sat, I could not say, but the sound of the front door creaking open snapped me to attention. For a moment I panicked, for I'd thought about what these "Dragon" aliens might do to me if they knew what I'd been told. But the sound of my wife and son tussling and bickering with each other brought me back to reality.

"We're home, honey," my wife called out.

I watched her enter the kitchen, looking around for me--so beautiful and simple a pleasure, to watch someone you love. I entered the kitchen, emotionally drained, but spiritually replenished.

Without a word, I wrapped my arms around my wife and squeezed.

Epilogue

That night was the last time I ever saw Azazel. Much of what he told me I have recorded here for the world to see. In memory of Azazel, a Halfling, but my friend. He risked his life and died to share information with me, and for that he is a hero. Now, I am returning the favor. I don't know the implications of what he has taught me, nor do I have any solutions to the problems that mankind will surely face in the coming generations. But someone reading might just have the answer. And for that reason, I will continue the task of sharing my story.

Bios

Amazon Queen

Amazonian warriors inhabit the planet Deva. In the earliest stages of life, they chose to live off the land. Their society is tribal; some would compare them to the Amish of North America, although their religious views resemble Taoism, which believes that both nature and humans are Chi (spirit-energy).

Amazonian warriors excel at mental control and manipulate nature to their advantage, although they do know how to use technological weapons such as the staff weapons as well. These beings often use little gray, native-born creatures as servants.

Amphibians

The Amphibians share the common ancestor of Hor. They spend most of their time in water; thus, their appearance mimics that of Earth amphibians, having webbed fingers and toes, and gills on their ribs or necks.

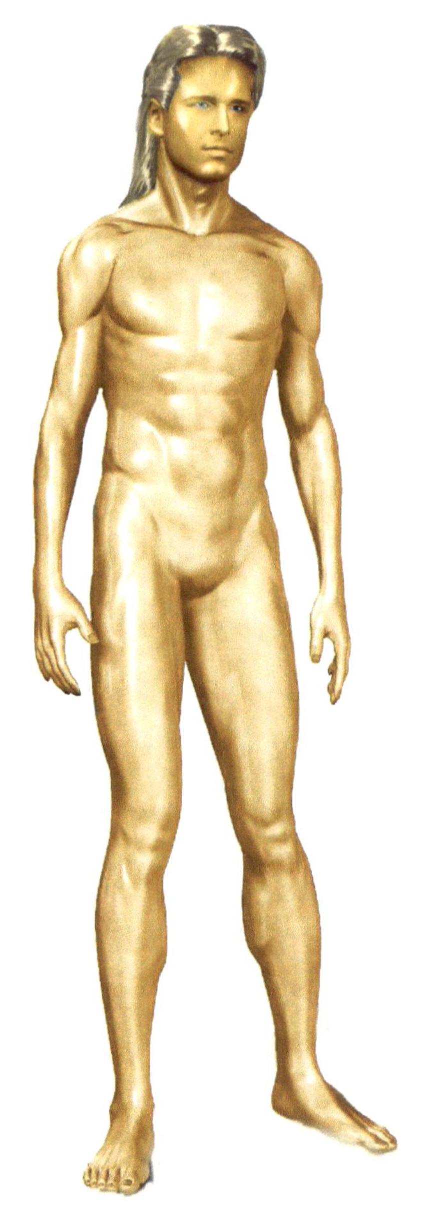

Anunnaki

Kingdom:	Animalia
Phylum:	Chordata
Class:	Mammalia
Genus:	**Homo**
Species:	*Homo titanese (large man)*

Slang names: Anunnaki – not to be confused with Nordics
Scientific name: *Homo titanese*
Distinguishing Marks: Large muscular body frame with a golden, Egyptian-like skin tone
Skin Type: Human
Skin Color: Golden hues
Eye Color: Human variations
Height: 6-9 feet
Weight: 250-500lbs
Origin: Unknown planet – 8 billion years ago

Evolution: The Anunnaki settled on a planet with a mass slightly more than that of Earth, and therefore possessing stronger gravitational force. The Anunnaki forced their own evolution with science, changing their DNA in order to make them larger and stronger.

History: Approximately 8 billion years ago, Architectus' race split into many factions on a variety of planets. On one of these planets, his race evolved into the Anunnaki. Using technology, the Anunnaki focused specifically on physical strength and size in order to become the ultimate warriors. Because of this, they are not as technologically or spiritually advanced as other races. Although their size and strength initially benefited them in war, the technology of other races inevitably rendered their anatomical strength obsolete. The Deva and Grays used technology to advance their minds, and they eventually unlocked hidden mental abilities such as ESP. This gave them the power to manipulate matter with their thoughts. Hence, these other derivations of Architectus' race gained a seemingly insurmountable advantage over the Anunnaki. The Anunnaki have since included the development of mind powers to their focus, but strength and weaponry still maintain their importance.

Respiratory system: Virtually identical to humans
Circulatory system: Virtually identical to humans
Reproductive system: Virtually identical to humans
Skeletal system: Virtually identical to humans
Muscular system: Virtually identical to humans
Digestive system: Virtually identical to humans

Diet: They do eat meat, but not often. Most advanced races take in food through pill or liquid form, as they usually receive more energy this way. However, some races indulge in the material world more than others and find that the consumption of food is still pleasurable.

Life Style: They live a lot like modern humans today, with much more advanced technology. They can be brutish and carnal in nature.

Art Mimicking Life: Klingons of Star Trek movies and television

Special Abilities: They have mental abilities such as ESP and Telekinesis, but have considerably less ability than other advanced races.

Weapons: "Laser" swords, although they don't look like the light sabers from Star Wars, having a more sword-like appearance. They do cut through objects as the light sabers. This glowing sword is specific to the Anunnaki. However, they also use conventional weapons like anti-gravity and cloaking devices, metal body suits and laser guns. Some of their weapons can destroy a whole city in one shot.

The Anunnaki use metal body suits as protection in combat situations. These suits look like paint-on latex, but are very strong. When fully garbed, the Anunnaki's suit appears metallic, which is why some who have seen them believe they have seen angels. This is also why in the Bible and other texts angels are said to have metal skin, like gold or bronze. As a side note, this suit can also give viewers the illusion that the Anunnaki are sexless, although this is not the case.

Density of tissue and functionality is subject to varying degrees of difference when compared to other races depending upon planetary conditions, atmospheric pressures, diet, etc.

Bigfoot

Slang names: Bigfoot, Yeti, Sasquatch
Distinguishing Marks: Large, hairy, ape-like
Skin Type: Human
Hair Color: Same as Humans
Eye Color: Usually brown
Height: around 7 feet
Weight: 500lbs
Origin: Some evolved on Earth, others on different planets
Short Story: People often see them on Reptilian ships, working as servants or cleaners.
Respiratory system: Same as humans
Circulatory system: Same as humans
Reproductive system: Same as humans
Skeletal system: Same as humans
Muscular system: Naturally strong
Digestive system: Same as humans
Diet: Similar to humans, with more meat consumption
Life Style: Unknown. These are private creatures, and stick close to brushy or woody areas.
Special Abilities: None

Chupacabra

Slang names: Chupacabra
Distinguishing Marks: Spikes on back
Skin Type: Hairy
Hair Color: Browns and reds
Eye Color: Red/yellow
Height: 2-3 feet tall
Weight: Unknown
Origin: Unknown planet
Evolution: Genetic alteration

Short story: It is uncertain what the Chupacabra is, but it has been seen with aliens in Mexico and Brazil. This species may be a type of pet or low-level worker, or an escaped military experiment. The name Chupacabra means "goat sucker," because they are often seen sucking on the necks of goats. They don't simply suck blood, though; they drain their victims, leaving two puncture wounds, similar to that of the famed vampire.

Respiratory system: Virtually identical to apes
Circulatory system: Virtually identical to apes
Reproductive system: Unknown
Skeletal system: Unknown
Muscular system: Virtually identical to apes
Digestive system: Virtually identical to apes
Diet: Blood
Life Style: Unknown
Special Abilities: None, although some witnesses claim they have low level mind- reading abilities.
Weapons: Their bodies

Deva

Kingdom:	Animalia
Phylum:	Chordata
Class:	Mammalia
Genus:	**Homo**
Species:	*Homo oculatuslongus (Lotus-eyed human)*

Slang names: The Hindus call them Deva, meaning "glowing or heavenly."
Scientific name: *Homo oculatuslongus*
Distinguishing Marks: Lotus-shaped eyes like the statue of Akhenaton
Skin Type: Human skin
Skin Color: Golden and blue hues. Not a true blue color, but more like a bluish tint over top of a golden skin color, like some Asians today, but more pronounced
Eye Color: Human eye colors, along with pale purple
Height: 4-6 feet tall, many on the shorter side of this
Weight: 90-250lbs
Origin: Unknown planet – 8 billion years ago
Evolution: The planet the Deva settled on is nearly identical to Earth. Pressure differences led to a difference in the Deva' blood chemistry, and a resulting increase in certain traits, including more blue hues in the skin, and eyes that grow longer and more slanted than humans.
Short story: Approximately 8 billion years ago, the Architectus race split into different factions on various planets through the universe. The Deva evolved from a faction of settlers. The Deva race devoutly keeps Architectus' philosophy alive, and practice it to this day.
Respiratory system: Virtually identical to humans
Circulatory system: Virtually identical to humans
Reproductive system: Virtually identical to humans
Skeletal system: Virtually identical to humans
Muscular system: Virtually identical to humans
Digestive system: Virtually identical to humans
Diet: They do not eat much, because their philosophy is not to care much about the material world or what can be seen with physical sight. They occasionally eat fruit.
Life Style: Some might compare the Deva way of life with that of monks in the Buddhist religion. They spend a lot of time in meditation, advancing their mental powers. They eat only to sustain a healthy body. It should be noted, however, that not all Deva live this lifestyle. In general, Deva are not so concerned with humans, although some of their children's descendants live on Earth.
Special Abilities: The Deva excel in the mental power of will, and can control technology with their minds.
Weapons: The Deva invented Mantra weapons, which use a mantra, or verbal password, to operate. All of their weapons use the power of the mind to control, including a spear-like weapon that shoots energy.

Although the Deva use mind-controlled weapons, they are taught how conventional bows and spears operate, since a race of more primitive creatures, the Amazons, live off of the land and utilize those kinds of weapons.

Density of tissue and functionality is subject to varying degrees of difference when compared to other races depending upon planetary conditions and atmospheric pressures, diet, etc.

Indra the Deva

Indra is a Hindu deity; however, he is also an extraterrestrial. In the Hindu texts (including the *Mahabharata*) he is described as the Emperor of three solar systems. As a Deva, he has eyes shaped as Lotus pedals and a light-golden skin color. He fights against the Dragon Empire.

On a side note to Indra, there was a time in history when Nahusha infiltrated Indra's kingdom, taking over as ruler for a time. When Indra reincarnated, however, he reclaimed his kingdom and sent Nahusha to Earth, where Nahusha became a serpent for 10,000 years. Nahusha was referred to in the Bible (Genesis, Chapter Three) as "Nachash," who deceived Eve in the Garden of Eden.

Going by the dates in the Bible, Nahusha has now served his 10,000 years and will inevitably have something large up his sleeve soon.

The painting is of a half-breed. Most hybrids only partially have the genetics of Grays.

Gray

Kingdom:	Animalia
Phylum:	Chordata
Class:	Mammalia
Order:	Primates
Genus:	*Homo*
Species:	*Homo sapien capito (large-headed human)*

Slang names: Grays, Greys

Scientific name: *Homo sapien capito*

Distinguishing Marks: Large cranium, especially the back of the skull

Skin Type: Although they do not have gray skin, some do have pale grayish-tinged skin, like the underside of a dolphin. It is said their skin feels clammy, similar to that of a dolphin, but smoother, like a human baby.

Skin Color: Movies have made popular a pale, grayish skin color, although Grays actually come in a variety of pale colors, including pink, blue, and human skin color.

Eye Color: Although images of Grays exaggerate the opaque black eyes, this is not a true representation of their features. Their eyes, in fact, resemble humans' more than anything. The black orbs are lenses that protect and extend the eyes' function. They block out UV light, bring out infrared, and zoom in and out like binoculars. They attach to the skin on a microscopic scale. The Grays control these lenses through simple thought.

Height: Usually 3-7 feet tall, although some have reported seeing Grays as tall as 7 feet. These taller variations are likely Hybrids, rather than full Grays.

Weight: 90-200lbs. Their muscles are far denser than ours, and this makes them slightly heavier by body mass ratio.

Origin: Unknown planet – 8 billion years ago

Evolution: Approximately 8 billion years ago, the Grays evolved on a distant planet. This planet had 4-5 times the force of gravity as Earth. Even with this difference, the Grays evolved into a species almost identical to *Homo sapiens*. However, the increased pressure resulted in shorter creatures that were better able to move on the heavy surface. Their technology developed quickly, and soon the Grays implanted themselves with brain chips. These chips forced natural selection to accommodate the abundance of information that could fit into their brains, and as a result of this, their brain size increased and new parts developed. Skull structure naturally increased as well. The spine centered more to hold up the large head, muscles became denser, and their fingers grew thinner and longer to work with smaller and smaller technological devices. The pinky virtually disappeared from lack of use, giving observers the illusion that the Grays have only three fingers. Since they used telepathy to communicate and didn't eat regularly, their jaws reduced in size.

Short story: Because the Grays spent most of their time perfecting their technology, they quickly drew recognition as the most advanced race; However, the Syn, created by the Sram (scaly reptoids), have developed enough to compete with the Grays. Philosophically speaking, the majority of Gray species lean towards agnosticism, which has led them to try to develop technologies to extend life. This has not quite worked as planned. Although they have managed to add thousands of years to their natural life through a process of "downloading" their thoughts and memories into a machine each night, they ultimately go mad with an overload of experience. Even as they develop new ways to deal with the problem, including transferring their memories into clones of themselves, and going through a virtual reality program every 1000 years or so to trick the mind, the problem still has not been solved, and eventually they must be put to sleep like a lame dog, once the haunting boogey-man of madness seizes them for good.

Respiratory: They breathe with lungs, as humans

Circulatory: Unknown, although it probably much different than humans

Sexual: There seems to be some confusion in this area. Some people believe that Grays have sexual organs; others say they don't. This mix-up is a result of there being two different species that share a similar appearance: the Grays and the Syn. The Syn are built and thus do not have sexual organs. The Grays do have sexual organs, but evolution has moved them inside the body. Women Grays can no longer have children through natural means; thus, females instead have children by artificial womb. The sperm of the male and the egg of the female are still used, but the child grows in an artificial womb. They still have belly buttons.

Diet: Grays do not eat typical food. Technology has created pieces of nutrition that can be consumed once every two to three days.

Life Style: The Africans, especially the Zulu tribe, speak a lot about this race. They call them *Mantindane*, "the Tormentor," although it is possible the Zulu are actually speaking of the Syn.

The Grays spend most of their time surrounded by advanced technology. There isn't much need for jobs anymore, as Nano-bots build everything they need; the main jobs that need filled are those that require high thought, such as inventors, scientists, explorers and peacekeepers.

Because they are not an inclusive race, they still have a government, which keeps them in competition with the Syn and allows them to fulfill their role as galactic peacekeepers, along with the Light Beings and Deva.

Special Abilities: Mind control. They excel at getting into the minds of less-advanced races, allowing them to access memories and influence them. They can paralyze others, through technology or mind control, and most are illusionists, convincing observers that they are not as they appear.

Weapons: They do not care much for weapons and have no need for them, although they have the technology to destroy planets.

Gray-Human

Slang names: Hybrid

Distinguishing Marks: Larger bald head, although some of them look human

Skin Type: Human

Hair Color: Same variations as humans

Eye Color: Usually the same as humans, although some have light purple eyes

Height: Shorter than the average human

Weight: Same or slightly heavier than humans

Origin: Hybrid projects are taking place on different planets.

Short story: Many contactees claim that Hybrids look so much like humans that they can pass as such, and often attend school, work and co-habitate with humans. Many hybrids have no idea what they are.

Respiratory system: Same as humans

Circulatory system: Same as humans

Reproductive system: Same as humans

Skeletal system: Same as humans

Muscular system: Naturally strong

Digestive system: Same as humans

Diet: Same as humans, although they are picky and often eat healthy.

Life Style: Similar to humans, although they seem to keep to themselves.

Special Abilities: Hybrids often have psychic abilities, and can usually finish other people's sentences or answer a question before it is asked. For their appearance, hybrids possess an abnormal level of strength. They are sensitive to UV light and ultra high/low pitches.

Humans who are born hybrid often don't realize their origin until well into their twenties. As children, hybrids often feel different, set apart somehow, even to the extent that they feel that something is wrong with them. Always the good student (if a little lax with the homework), hybrids usually take top honors in whatever pursuit they attempt. Adulthood can be consumed by trying to find out who they are, though memories of abduction experiences often help at this point.

Homoforma Reptilia

Homoforma Reptilia

Kingdom:	Animalia
Phylum:	Chordata
Class:	Dinosauria
Order:	Simiuscoxa (monkey hip)
Genus:	*Homoforma* (Human form)
Species:	*H. reptilia* (Homoforma reptiod)

Slang names: Reptilians

Scientific Name: *Homo reptilia*, **Hor** for short. This should replace the slang names, as Hor are not truly reptilians OR amphibians.

Distinguishing Marks: Marks exist on the back of their necks, bellies, and sometimes backs. I do not present the marks in this painting because Ufologists often use these as proof that a potential contactee has truly encountered a Hor.

Skin Type: Smooth and clammy, like that of a salamander

Skin Color: A mix of greens, yellows, reds, and browns. The skin usually has a greenish-brown tint as shown, with a yellowish-red belly. There are some natural variations.

Eye Color: Yellow-green, with a black-slit pupil

Height: 5-7 feet tall

Weight: 200-700lbs. This is an estimate based on body density. Keep in mind that a small person with more muscle can weigh more than a larger person because of body density.

Origin: Planet Earth – 75 MYA

Evolution: Hor evolved from the dinosaur species *Troodon.* The Anunnaki came to Earth around the time of the dinosaurs. They took the most intelligent dinosaur back for experimental purposes. Using their own DNA, the Anunnaki sped up the evolutionary process, eventually creating the *Homoforma Reptilia.*

Paleontologist Dale Russell, curator of vertebrate fossils at the National Museum of Canada in Ottawa, speculated in 1982 on how evolution would have proceeded if the Troodonts had survived the extinction of the dinosaurs. Russell speculated that a species like *Troodon* would have grown smarter and taken on a human-like appearance. Russell partnered with taxidermist and artist Ron Sequin and together they made a model of what a derived, intelligent *Troodon* would look like, naming their fantasy creation a "Dinosauroid". This might seem outlandish and downright ridiculous to those who do not have a working knowledge of how evolution works. According to the modern theory of evolution, humans evolved from a cousin to Troodon, the Oviraptor. Oviraptor looks similar in appearance to Troodon.

Short story: Approximately 10 million years after the Anunnaki used their DNA to advance the Troodon species, their creation, the Hor, became too intelligent to control. The Hor wanted to return to Earth and was granted the wish by the peacekeeping species, the Deva, who also made laws to protect them from harm. The Anunnaki did not like that idea and devised a plan to destroy Hor. About 65 million years ago, they directed a large meteorite to destroy the species. Since the Hor had highly developed psychic abilities, they felt the danger and moved underground. Instead of their demise, the meteorite nearly wiped out the entire realm of species on Earth. Still today, stories exist around the world, from India to Africa to the Americas, about Naga (snake-men) living underground.

In time, Hor developed enough technologically to leave Earth, and found other planets to settle. According to the ancient texts, they have the power to manipulate their appearance to mankind through

interrupting the brain's interpretation of what it sees. This isn't such a far-fetched idea, as we do this on a regular basis. The eyes see one thing but the brain interprets it as another.
Respiratory: Just as all reptiles, they breathe with lungs. Some abductees and contactees say Hor have the ability to breath underwater. Others report that the reptilians have a set of gills on their neck or rib area, which is feasible in the context of evolution.

Circulatory: Unknown

Sexual: Most have never developed exterior sexual organs, but reproduce through rubbing, as with other reptiles. There are stories that some of the Reptilians have intercourse and thus exterior sexual organs. The Hor birth amniotic eggs covered with leathery skin, although some appear to be placental.

Diet: Ancient texts support the idea that the Hor have a high vegetable/fruit diet. Mythology often brands them with the label of "baby-eater," although this is most unlikely. Hindu texts also claim that they cause miscarriages, but again, mankind often blames its gods for things that it cannot explain otherwise.

Life Style: The Hindu texts speak extensively on this topic. The Hor live on many planets, enjoying good food, dancing, conversations, and companionship. Some of them live a rather mundane human existence on Earth (of course, with some appearance manipulation, as previously explained).

The Hor who live on Earth will breed with only one race, seeing the mixing of races detestable. They also find religion detestable, believing rather in a Gnostic idea of reality, where an eternal intelligence, universally accessible and encouraging self-advancement, replaces the idea of God.

The Hor are very intelligent, but will not make a public affair of it. They often do well in all that they attempt, and enjoy science and technology.

I personally do not believe Hor live on earth; although, they might visit earth and remain here for short periods of time.

Human-Reptilian Hybrid

These hybrids look human, but often have a nasty side to them. They may be attracted at an early age to a magical cult, and must be monitored.

The painting is of a half-breed. Hybrids on earth look human and only have a small amount of reptilian DNA.

Krishna

Krishna was a human descended from an extraterrestrial bloodline. He had an awakened consciousness and could remember his past lives. This made him a powerful man. The ET often visited him and gave him their technology. It is said that Krishna had a slight blue hue to his skin, which is not unheard of across the continent of Asia.

Arjuna, taught by Krishna here and there, was abducted many times and received ET weapons. Arjuna's mother Kunti was human and his father was the ET Indra.

Mantis

Kingdom:	Animalia
Phylum:	Arthropoda
Class:	Unknown
Genus:	**Unknown**
Species:	*Unknown*

Slang names: Mantis
Scientific name: *Unknown*
Distinguishing Marks: They appear to have an exoskeleton.
Skin Type: Exoskeleton
Skin Color: Dark, sometimes black
Eye Color: Green, yellow, brown, black
Height: 5-7 feet
Weight: 250-500lbs
Origin: Unknown planet

Evolution: The existence of the Mantis is uncorroborated by ancient texts, but as is often the case, this does not imply that they did not exist. The Mantis may have evolved on a planet from Arthropoda. Here on Earth, large insects preceded the dinosaurs, which could indicate their existence.

Other possible explanations for the Mantis abound. Some say that aliens wearing advanced traveling suits may resemble the Mantis. In addition, the Reptilians could be using their mental powers to appear to look like the praying mantis.

Respiratory system: Unknown, probably through pores
Circulatory system: Unknown
Reproductive system: Unknown
Skeletal system: Exoskeleton
Muscular system: Unknown
Digestive system: Unknown
Diet: Conflicting reports, some claiming veggies, others claiming meat
Life Style: Unknown
Special Abilities: Claims of psychic ability
Weapons: Their bodies and technological weapons

Because I tend not to accept notions that I cannot support with enough evidence, I am unsure the Mantis exists. I prefer to think that they are reptilians wearing advanced armor.

Marduk

To read a famous story about Marduk, check out the *Enuma Elish*; it is a rather short, seven-tablet story. In this story, Marduk is sent to kill Tiamat, the goddess ET ruler of the Anunnaki, who has pushed her kind into a terrible, toiling lifestyle. Marduk succeeds in his task, and may or may not have created man by mixing his blood with that of an Earth primate.

Mothman

Slang names: Mothman.
Scientific name: None.
Distinguishing Marks: Red eyes, wings.
Skin Type: Furry, like a bat.
Skin Color: Dark brown.
Eye Color: Glowing red.
Height: 6-8 feet tall.
Weight: Unknown.
Origin: This is one of the forms that the Reptilians put into human minds.

Short story: Reptilians are known to project themselves differently in the minds of humans, and the Mothman is most likely one of these projections. Reptilians, especially in the Hindu texts, are known to take forms to invoke a sense of fear. A winged beast with wild red eyes does just that.

Nordic

Kingdom:	Animalia
Phylum:	Chordata
Class:	Mammalia
Genus:	**Homo**
Species:	*Homo procerus (Tall man)*

Slang names: Nordic, Pleiadians
Scientific name: *Homo procerus.*
Distinguishing Marks: Tall and thin.
Skin Type: Human skin.
Skin Color: Light skinned.
Eye Color: Blue, ice blue, ice green.
Height: 6-7 feet tall.
Weight: 160-180lbs.
Origin: Unknown planet – Unknown time.

Evolution: At an unknown time, the Nordics evolved into a tall, thin race. Certain tribes in Africa have evolved into tall, thin races as well, so we know that Earth has the proper pressures and conditions to cause such an evolution. Nordics might originally come from Earth, were taken by one of the other races, and evolved from that point on. If the race already had genetic coding to grow tall, and they were taken to a planet with less gravity, there is a good chance the race would grow even taller.

Short story: People don't know a lot about the Nordics, since they are not found in the ancient texts. In fact, Nordics are a pretty new arrival on the scene.

Respiratory: They breathe through lungs.
Circulatory: Same as humans.
Sexual: Same as humans.
Diet: Unknown, but most eat the same things as humans.
Life Style: They live a lot like humans, but with advanced technology.
Special Abilities: Mental abilities, including telepathy.
Weapons: Unknown, although it is clear that they use telepathy and manipulation as a weapon.

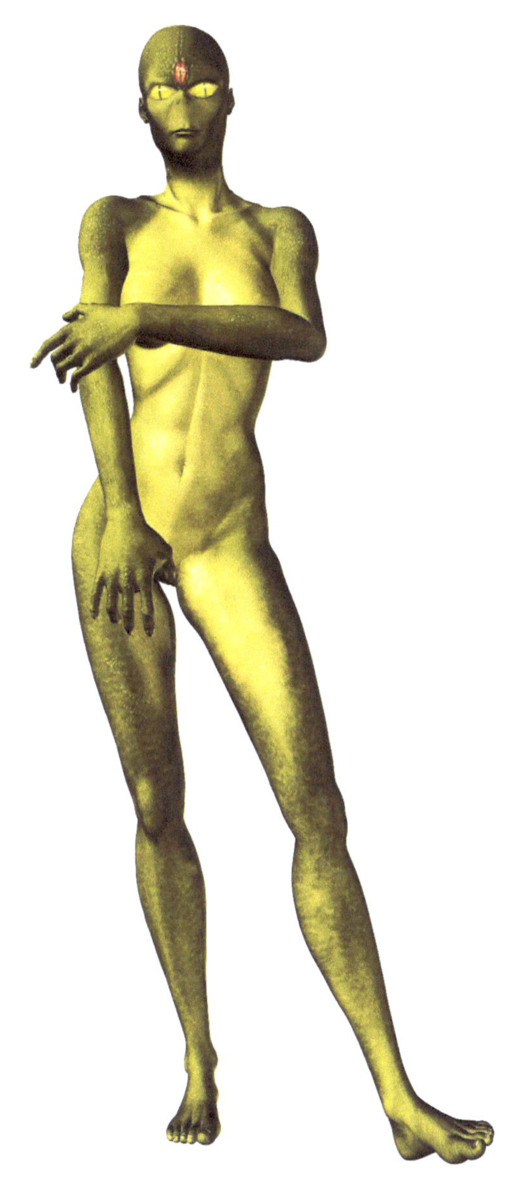

Homosquamosus *reptilian*

Kingdom:	Animalia
Phylum:	Chordata
Class:	Sauropsida
Order:	Simislacerta (monkey lizard)
Genus:	*Homosquamosus (Scaly man)*
Species:	*Homosquamosus reptilia (Scaly reptile man)*

Slang names: Reptilians, Chitauli, Sram

Scientific name: *Homosquamosus reptilia.*

Distinguishing Marks: Some have a third, red eye, others have a crown of horns like Darth Sidious from Star Wars.

Skin Type: Scaly, with the feel of a chicken leg.

Skin Color: Hues of green, yellow, red, and brown. On the extremities, the skin is usually a brownish-green, but the belly is usually a yellowish-red. Some natural variations occur.

Eye Color: Yellow-green, with a black-slit pupil. The third eye is reddish.

Height: 5-7 feet tall.

Weight: 200-800lbs. This is an estimate based on body density. Keep in mind that a smaller person with more muscle can weigh more than a larger person because of body density.

Origin: Unknown planet – 6 BYA.

Evolution: Approximately 6 billion years ago on a distant planet, creatures similar to Sauropsida (the ancestors of modern reptiles) lived. This branch evolved into *Simislacerta* (monkey lizard), a 2-foot-tall creature with both monkey and reptilian features. From this branch, the *Homosquamosus* evolved, a species similar to Homo erectus on Earth, the difference being in their reptilian characteristics. The 'third eye' of the *Homosquamosus* resulted from the standard pineal gland that reptiles have in their skulls. This third eye, which functions as a light indicator and helps calibrate the internal clock in Reptilians, slowly migrated towards the forehead, and eventually evolved into a basic eye. The purpose remained the same, and new purposes developed. Reptilians can see in the light spectrum, which includes the infrared.

Short story: Once Sram became a technological species, they began an intense competition with the Grays, who were more advanced than them. Jealous that they were not the dominant race, they sent scouts to steal some of the Grays' DNA. Using nano-bot technology, the Sram built a biological android, named Syn, short for Synthetic. It is the Syn that brought Sram into immediate contention with the Grays, and the battle between the two species continues today. Many contactees mistakenly think the Syn are Grays.

Respiratory: They breathe using lungs.

Circulatory: Unknown.

Sexual: Most have never developed exterior sexual organs and reproduce through rubbing instead of intercourse. Some of the Reptilians, however, do have intercourse, and thus external sexual organs. Birth is by amniotic eggs covered in leathery skin, although some appear to be placental.

Diet: Their diet is less understood than Hor. They appear to eat a lot of meat.

Life Style: The Africans, especially the Zulu tribe, speak a lot about this race. Legends report the existence of the third red eye, and the Hindus, who also have legends about Sram, seem to incorporate this third eye in their culture. Sram often abduct humans to conduct hybrid experiments.

Special Abilities: They are not as gifted as the Grays at mind reading, but they can shape-shift, or alter how others perceive them.

Weapons: Sram use conventional weapons, because their mind-control powers are not strong enough to utilize mind-control weapons.

Stitch

I have named this creature Stitch because of its resemblance to a creature from a modern cartoon. It appeared to two farm families one night in 1955, Billy Ray Taylor and Lucky Sutton. Apparently, Taylor relayed the story to the Suttons that he had seen a UFO with rainbow-colored exhaust. The Suttons, of course, refused to believe him. About thirty minutes later, however, both Taylor and Sutton saw the creature. They both fired at it, and the creature fell over briefly. It then stood and scurried away. Throughout the night, the two farmers shot at a few more of the creatures, finally going to the police for help. The police found nothing and left. Not long after, Stitch and his friends returned to stare through the windows of these country friends. They were never hostile, and the farmers involved never profited, nor did they ever try to, from the visit, which serves to validate that it could really have happened.

Syn

Kingdom:	Animansarchitectus (Invented life)
Phylum:	Chordatarchitectus
Class:	Absumgenus (No children)
Genus:	**Scoeo**
Species:	*Scoeo gene* (Assembled genes)

Slang names: Gray (mistakenly), Syn

Scientific name: *Scoeo gene*

Distinguishing Marks: Large cranium, especially the backside. Their heads are larger than the Grays.

Skin Type: Soft, nearly transparent mammalian skin, similar to the human baby. Pink and blue tones appear to move through an almost-transparent skin. It is similar to the rainbow colors seen when oil floats on top of water.

Skin Color: Pale in color.

Eye Color: Opaque black eyes are actually lenses that cover quite human-looking eyes. The black orbs are lenses that protect and extend the eyes' function. They block out UV light, bring out infrared, and zoom in and out like binoculars. They attach to the skin on a microscopic scale.

Height: 3-5 feet tall.

Weight: Because they are synthetic, their weight is hard to judge. They use anti-gravity technology anyway, and contactees usually see them floating across the ground, like a ghost.

Origin: Unknown planet – 5 billion years ago.

Evolution: Approximately five billion years ago, the Sram created Syn using nano-bot technology.

Short story: Even though they were created by the Sram, they have since broken from their creators, remaining loyal to them at the same time. They have a high interest in humanoids, in particular how humans express emotion and attempt to understand the universe.

Respiratory: They have lungs.

Circulatory: Unknown. It is likely their blood chemistry is much different than humans.

Sexual: They do not reproduce. Instead, they synthetically create themselves.

Diet: They sleep in a vitamin-rich liquid.

Life Style: Fast paced, utilizing every moment of the day. They study humanoids in order to understand emotions, and work to increase their technological capabilities. They have an intense interest in religion and spiritual matters.

Special Abilities: Mind reading.

Weapons: Advanced conventional weapons, and mind-control weapons. They do not yet have the skills of the Deva and Grays.

Glossary

Akhenaten – An Egyptian Pharaoh first known as Amenhotep IV.

Alternoanima – The fictional name of the planet where Architectus was born.

Amphibians – Reptiod extraterrestrials with aquatic features.

Anunnaki – Large humanoid extraterrestrials. Also called Titans, Niphilim, Danavas, and Daityas in ancient texts.

Architectus – A fictional name for the first man that entered into the test for eternal life.

BYA – Billion Years Ago.

Chupacabra – In Spanish it means *goat sucker*. The vampire-like creature seen most often in Central and South America.

DE – Dragon Empire, started by Satan.

Deva – Humanoid extraterrestrials with lotus-pedal shaped eyes.

Ea – (Yah) An Anunnaki.

Enuma Elish – Seven Babylonian tablets that describe the creation of the universe and humans.

Epic of Gilgamesh – Eleven Sumerian Tablets.

ESS – Egyptian Secret Society, started by Ra.

Hor – Slang for Human Form Reptiod.

Indra – A Deva and King of the galaxy.

Mahabharata – A Hindu holy text dating to about 800BC.

Marduk – An Anunnaki, the son of Ea.

Nano-bots – Microscopic robots that can assemble and disassemble matter, and are often utilized by extraterrestrials.

Nordics – Large, blond humanoid extraterrestrials. Also called Pleiadians.

Ra – An Anunnaki extraterrestrial.

Ramayana – A Hindu text dating between 800-500BC.

SB – Srimad Bhagavatam – A Hindu text written about 1000BC, with the oldest copy dating to 1000AD.

Sram – The slang term for **Homosquamosus *reptilia.***

Syn – Short for Synthetic.

Tiamat – An Anunnaki female.

UFO – Unidentified Flying Object.

Ultra-galaxy – What we call the known universe. There are googolplexes of ultra-galaxies in the actual universe.

Wormhole – A warping of space-time that forms a tunnel, usually used as a shortcut from point A to point B.

Yhwh – The name of the OT god or ET.

www.ingramcontent.com/pod-product-compliance
Lightning Source LLC
LaVergne TN
LVHW070141110826
845147LV00002B/299
9780615189109